Read Me Another Story

Frank Waters

Beaver Books

First published in 1976
under the title *More Reading with Mother* by
George G. Harrap & Company Limited
182–184 High Holborn, London WC1V 7AX

This paperback edition published in 1978 by
The Hamlyn Publishing Group Limited
London · New York · Sydney · Toronto
Astronaut House, Feltham, Middlesex, England

© Copyright George G. Harrap &
Company Limited 1976
ISBN 0 600 37607 9

Printed in England by
Cox & Wyman Limited
London, Reading and Fakenham
Set in Monotype Plantin Light

Editor's Note

The contents of this volume have the same purpose as that of its predecessor, *Read Me a Story* – to entertain any child who has begun to read, with the assumption that a helpful adult is at hand either to supervise his efforts or to read the stories and verse aloud. The upper age limit of the child is difficult to determine, but it is assumed to be approximately seven: there is virtually no lower age limit, the only criterion being that the material must arouse and hold the child's interest.

I would like to take this opportunity of expressing my particular pleasure at the inclusion of two items. First, one of Michael Flanders' animal lyrics. He was a marvellously modest and gracious person who, with better health, would have left behind him a collection of comic verse that would have been unrivalled. Several times I seem to have got him to the brink, but his stamina failed him. He laughingly brushed aside the difficulties by saying that he was by nature incurably lazy and that his wheel chair life suited him perfectly.

Secondly, the story by Jane Barry – and, indeed, her illustrations to the story and that of her mother Margaret Stuart Barry. Jane is surely bound to go far in life, unless her interest flags (which would be a tragedy). At the age of twelve she sold a short story to the B.B.C., and at the same age she was displaying a most original talent for illustration; and to this she has now added – amidst studying for A-levels – a musical competence which is, to say the least, very promising. Her story in this book was written and illustrated when she was fourteen and fifteen, and is a classic example of an original comic mind at work. When I compare it with the hundreds of dull, painstaking efforts of adults 'writing for children' which land on my desk each year I am amazed. I only hope this little public praise will act as an incentive to her in the years to come.

I am also indebted to the following for permission to

include material in this book: Messrs Gerald Duckworth and Co. Ltd for 'Rebecca' from *Cautionary Tales* by Hilaire Belloc and the illustrations by B.T.B.; The Estate of Lord Dunsany for 'The Wind in the Wood'; Messrs. Faber and Faber Ltd for 'The Old Gumbie Cat' by T. S. Eliot from *Old Possum's Book on Practical Cats*; and to the same publishers for 'Tim Rabbit and the Scissors' from *The Adventures of No Ordinary Rabbit* by Alison Uttley; Messrs. Chappell and Co. Ltd for 'The Hippopotamus Song' by Michael Flanders; The Society of Authors as the Literary Representatives of the Estate of Rose Fyleman for 'Mice'; Lady Herbert for 'The Spider' from *The Wherefore and the Why* by A. P. Herbert; The late Mrs George Bambridge and The Macmillan Company of London and Basingstoke for the poem, 'The Hump' from *Just So Stories* by Rudyard Kipling; Methuen's Children's Books Ltd and Messrs. McClelland and Stewart Ltd for 'Halfway Down' from *When we were very Young* by A. A. Milne, and for the accompanying illustration by E. H. Shepard; Messrs. George G. Harrap and Co. Ltd, and the Executors of Arthur Rackham for the illustrations to 'The Night Before Christmas'; and to the authors Margaret Stuart Barry, Elizabeth Robinson, Francis Mott and R. J. Parker for allowing me to include original work for this compilation.

Contents

THE THREE GOATS
NAMED GRUFF

Once upon a time there were three goats named Gruff
that were going to the mountain pasture to fatten. On the
road there was a bridge across a waterfall over which they
had to pass, and under which lived a great ugly ogre with
eyes as large as tin plates, and a nose as long as a
broomstick.

The youngest goat came first on the bridge.

'*Trip trap, trip trap*,' said the bridge as he went over.

'Who trips on my bridge?' cried the ogre.

'Oh! it is only the little goat Gruff. I am going to the
mountain pasture to get fat,' said the goat in a soft voice.

'I am coming to catch you,' said the ogre.

'Oh! no, pray don't take me, for I am so little; but if
you will wait, the second goat Gruff is coming in a
minute, and he is much bigger.'

'Be it so,' said the ogre.

Soon the second goat came passing over the bridge.

'*TRIP TRAP, TRIP TRAP, TRIP TRAP,*' said the bridge.

'Who trips over my bridge?' cried the ogre.

'Oh! it is the second goat Gruff, who is going to the mountain-pasture to get fat,' said the goat in a deeper voice.

'I am coming to catch you,' said the ogre.

'Oh! no, pray don't take me. Wait a moment; the big goat Gruff is only just behind me: he is much, much bigger than I am.'

'Be it so,' answered the ogre.

Just at that moment came the big goat Gruff upon the bridge.

'*TRIP TRAP, TRIP TRAP, TRIP TRAP,*' said the bridge; he was so heavy that the bridge creaked and cracked under him.

'Who goes tramping on my bridge?' roared the ogre.

'It is I, the great goat Gruff!' said the goat, who had a very deep voice.

'I am coming to catch you,' cried the ogre, and jumped upon the bridge.

'You're welcome,' said the big goat, and without more ado he rushed upon the ogre, broke his bones, and with his horns thrust him over into the waterfall. He then trotted on to the pasture as though nothing had happened.

There the three billy goats grew so fat, so fat, that they were hardly able to walk home from the pasture, and snip, snap, snout, now my story's out.

The Night Before Christmas

'Twas the night before Christmas, when all through the
house,
Not a creature was stirring, not even a mouse;
The stockings were hung by the chimney with care,
In hopes that St Nicholas soon would be there;
The children were nestled all snug in their beds,
While visions of sugar-plums danced in their heads;

And mamma in her kerchief, and I in my cap,
Had just settled our brains for a long winter's nap; –
When out on the lawn there arose such a clatter,
I sprang from my bed to see what was the matter.
Away to the window I flew like a flash,
Tore open the shutters and threw up the sash.
The moon on the breast of the new-fallen snow,

Gave the lustre of midday to objects below,
When, what to my wondering eyes should appear,
But a miniature sleigh and eight tiny reindeer,
With a little old driver, so lively and quick,
I knew in a moment it must be St Nick.

More rapid than eagles his coursers they came,
And he whistled and shouted, and called them by name:
    'Now, *Dasher!* now, *Dancer!* now, *Prancer!* and
    Vixen!
On, *Comet!* on, *Cupid!* on, *Donner* and *Blitzen!*
To the top of the porch! to the top of the wall!
Now dash away! dash away! dash away all!'

As dry leaves that before the wild hurricane fly,
When they meet with an obstacle, mount to the sky;
So up to the house-top the coursers they flew
With the sleigh full of toys and St Nicholas too.
And then, in a twinkling, I heard on the roof
The prancing and pawing of each little hoof –
As I drew in my head, and was turning around,

Down the chimney St Nicholas came with a bound.
He was dressed all in furs from his head to his foot,
And his clothes were all tarnished with ashes and soot;
A bundle of toys he had flung on his back,
And he looked like a pedlar just opening his pack.
His eyes – how they twinkled! his dimples – how
merry!

His cheeks were like roses, his nose like a cherry!
His droll little mouth was drawn up like a bow,
And the beard on his chin was as white as the snow;
The stump of a pipe he held tight in his teeth,
And the smoke it encircled his head like a wreath;
He was chubby and plump, a right jolly old elf;
And I laughed when I saw him, in spite of myself;
A wink of his eye and a twist of his head

Soon gave me to know I had nothing to dread;
He spoke not a word, but went straight to his work
And filled all the stockings; then turned with a jerk,
And laying his finger aside of his nose,
And giving a nod, up the chimney he rose.

He sprang to his sleigh, to his team gave a whistle
And away they all flew like the down of a thistle.
But I heard him exclaim, ere he drove out of sight,
'*Happy Christmas to all, and to all a good night !*'

Clement C. Moore

Hey, Diddle, Diddle

Hey, diddle, diddle, the cat and the fiddle,
The cow jumped over the moon;
The little dog laughed to see such sport,
And the dish ran away with the spoon.

Humpty-Dumpty

Humpty-Dumpty sat on a wall,
   Humpty-Dumpty had a great fall;
All the King's horses, and all the King's men,
   Couldn't put Humpty together again.

The Wind in the Wood

In the hut of the mushroom-picker near Slumber Wood
was a child named Amelia Ann. When there was plenty
of time on hand and no work to be done she used to be
called Amelia, but in times of hurry she was called Ann.
And one day her parents went out to gather mushrooms,
leaving her alone in the hut, and warning her before they
went to keep a sharp look-out for wolves and not to stray
far from the door. There had been no wolves near their
hut for a hundred years, but they had learned about the
wood and the world from their grandfathers, and noticed
that they had known more about both than the folks of
the present day knew, and these grandfathers had always
warned them against wolves, so they taught their child
accordingly. And as soon as they had gone Amelia, who
knew that there were no wolves, went away by herself to

the wood. Hunger drove her parents afield, and curiosity drove Amelia, and so they hastily went their separate ways. When Amelia came to the very deep of the wood she had scarce gone far through the dark of it when she came on a dim blue figure fifty feet high, sitting up hunched on the moss and not so opaque as to hide the trunks of the trees.

'Who are you?' said Amelia, though she knew it at once for the wind.

And the wind without any concealment told her gladly who he was, with a loud shrill voice that sounded amused and excited.

'What are you going to do?' said Amelia.

And at that the wind seemed torn and wracked by dilemma. To begin with he was bubbling over to tell her, but then what he had to tell was so huge and delightful a secret that it seemed a pity to spoil it by sharing it with a soul, and then again he wanted to tell it because it seemed to splendid, and then again he didn't. But in the end he had to tell it to someone. So he looked round left and right, to see that no one was listening, and to show what a great secret it was; then he leaned forward and rubbed his hands and said: 'I am going to blow!'

'How jolly,' said Amelia.

'To blow!' said the wind.

'I thought you would,' said Amelia.

Not a grass-blade stirred, not a leaf swayed on its stem, in the deep dead hush of the wood.

'How did you know?' said the wind.

'By the look of the sky,' she answered.

The wind gave a sudden surprised look up at the sky, disappointed that there should be anywhere any hint of his secret. Sure enough there were little clouds wearing a wild look, but the wind turned contemptuously away from them.

'Yes, I am going to blow,' he said.

'What are you going to blow?' said Amelia.

'Leaves,' said the wind.

'And ships?' asked Amelia.

With a hand the colour of a wintry sky he rubbed the mighty shadows about his chin. He did not like the question. With the cunning of sails he had found himself put to uses.

'No, leaves,' he said.

'Which way will you blow them?' she asked.

And suddenly he spoke as though he were wiser than she, and as though behind his words was the wisdom of ages. 'That depends on which way I come out of the wood,' he said.

'And which way will you?' she asked.

'Ah,' he said.

'That way?' asked Amelia, pointing to the wind's right.

'If I go that way,' he said, 'I shall be a North wind.'

'Or that way?' she asked, pointing behind her.

'If I go that way,' he said, 'I shall be a West wind.'

'Be a West wind,' she said.

'Why?' he asked.

'Because a West wind is funny,' she said. 'The North wind is angry, and nobody likes an East wind. Be a West wind.'

'Perhaps,' he said.

'Or a South.'

'We shall see,' he said.

'Will you blow them hard?' asked Amelia.

28

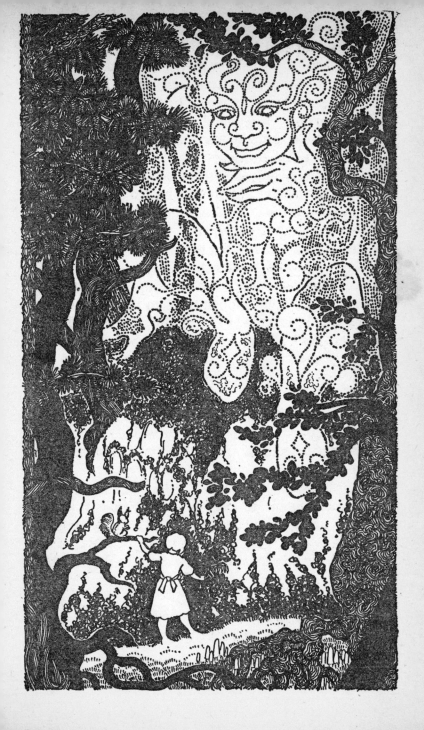

'Whew!' he said.

'How hard will you blow them?' she asked him.

'I'll dance them round and round for a bit,' he said. 'Then, when I leave the wood, I'll make them run.'

'And what else will you blow?' she asked.

'Ha,' he said. And the whole wood rang with his glee.

'Twigs?' asked Amelia.

'Whole trees,' answered the wind. 'But that's not all.' And all the wood was aware that he had a secret.

'You'll blow the wild geese south,' she guessed.

'Better than that,' said he.

'You'll blow icebergs out to sea?'

'Ha, ha,' he said. 'Better than that.'

And while she sat and wondered, a kind of twinkle seemed rippling up through the dim blue bulk of that figure. Partly it seemed like starlight, and partly like laughter. And all the wood was hushed. He seemed a jolly fellow. A delightful possibility crossed her mind. But she could not be sure, and it was better to ask.

'What then?' she said.

'I shall go to the towns,' said the wind.

'And then?' said Amelia, her merry suspicions closer now on his secret.

And the twinkles increased in the wind. And, just as he seemed unable to keep his secret in any longer, Amelia asked him again: 'What will you blow then?'

And the wind shouted his answer in the deep hush of the trees.

'Hats,' he bawled gleefully.

'I thought you would,' said Amelia.

'Hats through the streets,' he shouted.

30

'Oh, what fun, what fun,' said Amelia. And together they went out romping, through the western side of the wood.

Lord Dunsany

Rebecca

WHO SLAMMED DOORS FOR FUN AND PERISHED MISERABLY

A Trick that everyone abhors
In Little Girls is slamming Doors.
A

Wealthy Banker's

Little Daughter

Who lived in Palace Green, Bayswater
(By name Rebecca Offendort),
Was given to this Furious Sport.

She would deliberately go

And Slam the door
  like Billy-Ho!

To make

her

Uncle Jacob start.

She was not really bad at heart,
But only rather rude and wild:
She was an aggravating child. . . .

It happened that a Marble Bust
Of Abraham was standing just
Above the Door this little Lamb
Had carefully prepared to Slam,
And Down it came! It knocked her flat!

It laid her out! She looked
                        like that.

Her funeral Sermon (which was long
And followed by a Sacred Song)
Mentioned her Virtues, it is true,
But dwelt upon her Vices too,
And showed the Dreadful End of One
Who goes and slams the door for Fun.

The children who were brought to hear
The awful Tale from far and near
Were much impressed,

and inly swore
They never more would slam the Door.
– As often they had done before.

Hilaire Belloc

Solomon Grundy

Solomon Grundy,
Born on a Monday,
Christened on Tuesday,
Married on Wednesday,
Very ill on Thursday,
Worse on Friday,
Died on Saturday,

Buried on Sunday.
This is the end
Of Solomon Grundy.

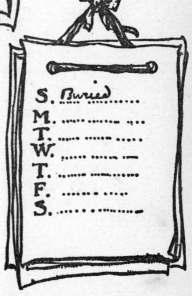

Twinkle, Twinkle, Little Star,

Twinkle, twinkle, little star,
How I wonder what you are!
Up above the world so high,
Like a diamond in the sky.

When the blazing sun is gone,
When he nothing shines upon,
Then you show your little light,
Twinkle, twinkle, all the night.

Then the traveller in the dark
Thanks you for your tiny spark:
How could he see where to go,
If you did not twinkle so?

In the dark blue sky you keep,
Often through my curtains peep,
For you never shut your eye,
Till the sun is in the sky.

As your bright and tiny spark
Lights the traveller in the dark,
Though I know not what you are,
Twinkle, twinkle, little star.

Jane Taylor

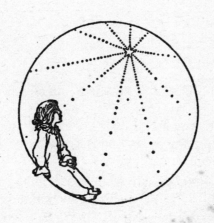

Goosey, Goosey, Gander

Goosey, goosey, gander, whither shall I wander?
Up stairs, and down stairs, and in my lady's chamber.

There I met an old man, who would not say his prayers,
I took him by his left leg, and threw him down the stairs.

The Real Princess and the Pea

Once upon a time there was a prince, and he wanted a princess; but she would have to be a *real* princess. He travelled all round the world to find one, but always there was something wrong. There were princesses enough, but he found it difficult to make out whether they were *real* ones. There was always something about them that was not quite right. So he came home again and was very sad, for he would have liked very much to have a real princess.

One evening a terrible storm came on; it thundered and lightninged, and the rain poured down in torrents. It was really dreadful! Suddenly knocking was heard at the city gate, and the old King himself went to open it.

It was a princess standing out there before the gate. But, good gracious! what a sight she was after all the rain and the dreadful thunder! The water ran down from her hair and her clothes; it ran down into the toes of her shoes and out again at the heels. And yet she said that she was a real princess.

'Yes, we'll soon find that out,' thought the old Queen. But she said nothing, went into the bedroom, took all the bedding off the bedstead, and laid a pea at the bottom; then she took twenty mattresses and laid them on the pea, and then twenty eiderdowns on top of the mattresses.

On this the Princess was to lie all night. In the morning she was asked how she had slept.

'Oh, terribly badly!' said the Princess. 'I have scarcely shut my eyes the whole night. Heaven only knows what was in the bed, but I was lying on something hard, so that I am black and blue all over my body. It is really terrible!'

Now they knew that she was a real princess, because she had felt the pea right through the twenty mattresses and the twenty eiderdowns.

Nobody but a real princess could be as sensitive as that.

So the prince took her for his wife, for he now knew that he had a real princess; and the pea was put in the Art Museum, where it may still be seen, if no one has stolen it.

There, that is a real story!

Mole Discovers a Coal Mine

Hare came bounding lollopy-gallopy along The Pathway by Rippling Stream. On his head he wore a postman's peaked cap, and he carried a canvas mailbag slung over his shoulder. Written on the bag in bold blue letters were the words:

HARE ESQ. POSTMAN AND MESSENGER

He stopped to breakfast on the juicy bark of a young willow. There was a flash of blue, and Kingfisher perched by Hare's nose. 'Morning, Hare,' he said.

'Mornin', Kingfisher,' Hare replied. 'Is there any news?' For Kingfisher heard all the news. Little escaped him as he sped swiftly hither and thither.

'Owl's Oak is to come down,' said Kingfisher. 'I heard some men talking about it. And Hedgehog is awake.'

'It's a pity about Owl's Oak,' said Hare. 'But I'm pleased about Hedgehog. I've missed him. Why he wants to sleep the winter away beats me. Well, I must be off. Goo'-bye, Kingfisher.'

Kingfisher dived like a streak of blue ribbon into Rippling Stream, and returned to his perch with a fish in his long beak. He tossed it into the air, then swallowed it down head first. 'Good-bye, Hare,' he called, in a just-swallowed-a-whole-fish sort of voice.

Hare came to The Wildwood, and pushed his way through the undergrowth until he reached the gaping entrance to Badger's house. Tripping over a pile of dry leaves and bracken, he tumbled headlong into Badger's fusty, dusty living-room.

Badger was snoozing in a fat, over-stuffed armchair

by his fireplace. He rose in alarm. 'Oh, it's you, Hare! You startled me,' he grumbled.

'Sorry to come burstin' in, Badger,' Hare apologised. 'I tripped over that pile of rubbish in your doorway.'

'Rubbish!' growled Badger. 'That isn't rubbish, Hare. That is my winter bedding put out to air.'

Hare looked embarrassed. 'Sorry, Badger. I've come with a message for you, from Mrs Mole.'

Badger looked pleased. 'A message, Hare. What is it?'

Hare slapped his forehead with a large forepaw. 'There now. I've gone and forgotten it!' he exclaimed vexedly. 'But I shall remember it, Badger, if you give me time. I'm very thirsty. Please may I have a drink?'

'Help yourself,' Badger invited. 'There's a bucket of water in the corner, and you'll find a cup on the dresser.'

Hare took a cup, and blew the dust from it. 'What a mess!' he scolded. 'Dust everywhere.'

'Don't fuss, Hare,' said Badger lazily. 'Dormouse will soon wake from her winter sleep. She will clean my house for me.'

Hare dipped the cup into a bucket of water, and drank thirstily.

'Not that bucket, Hare!' Badger cried in alarm. 'It has my best collection of water-bugs in it. I shall be most upset if you have swallowed any of them.'

'So shall I,' said Hare, and he hiccuped uneasily.

The shock of probably having swallowed some of Badger's water-bugs made Hare remember the message. 'Mrs Mole says she has the screws you ordered,' he told Badger. 'What do you want with screws, Badger?'

'I'm going to build a book-case, and put my book in it,' Badger replied proudly.

'A book-case, for one book,' Hare scoffed.

Badger looked annoyed. 'I intend to buy more books,' he said testily. 'Education is a fine thing, Hare. A very fine thing. Now be a good fellow, and run and fetch my screws.'

As Hare bounded lollopy-gallopy in the direction of Mrs Mole's shop, he thought that Badger had never been quite the same since he found that book about water-bugs left by a picnicker on the banks of Rippling Stream. Badger had always fancied himself, of course; but now he was quite impossible, with all his talk of education.

Mrs Mole's shop was tucked away among the bracken in a corner of The Wildwood. It had white bow windows on either side of a white door. Hare had to stoop to enter.

Mrs Mole, wearing a pink frilled cap and apron, stood behind the counter. While she was searching short-sightedly for the screws among a jumble of this and that, Hare said, 'I haven't seen Mole lately, Mrs Mole. I trust he is well.'

'Yes, Hare, very well thank you. He is in business himself now, you know,' Mrs Mole replied proudly. 'He has found a coal mine.'

'A coal mine!' Hare exclaimed. 'Well, I never.'

On his way back to Badger's house, Hare saw Mole, with Hedgehog. Hedgehog was standing by a little handcart, and leaning on a besom, for he was the road-sweeper. Mole was talking excitedly.

Hare stopped. 'Mornin', Hedgehog. I trust you've had an enjoyable sleep.'

'A most enjoyable sleep, thank you, Hare,' Hedgehog replied.

Hare turned to Mole. 'Mornin', Mole. I hear you've found a coal mine.'

Mole puffed out his black velvet chest. 'Yes, Hare. I was just telling Hedgehog. I discovered it at the end of one of my tunnels. You know what this means, Hare: I shall be rich. Rich! What do you think of that, eh?' He scurried away.

Hedgehog grinned. 'Mole always was an excitable fellow,' he said. 'But I don't suppose the coal mine will be any more successful than Mole's other ventures.' He curled himself into a ball and rolled over to spear some toffee papers on his spines. 'There are some very untidy people about, Hare,' he said, as he uncurled himself. 'Now tell me what has been happening while I've been asleep.'

The two stood gossiping for a while, until Hare remembered Badger's screws. 'Good-bye, Hedgehog,' he said. 'I must dash.'

'Good-bye Hare,' said Hedgehog. He picked up his besom, and began to sweep The Pathway.

Badger took the screws eagerly. 'Thank you, Hare. Would you care to stay and help me to build my bookcase?'

'Sorry, Badger, I haven't time, I have to clear the letter box,' Hare replied.

The letter box was a hole in the trunk of a crab-apple tree, and in it Hare found enough letters to keep him busy for the rest of the morning.

Late that afternoon, as he hurried along The Pathway, on his way to see how Badger was progressing with his bookcase, Hare saw Hedgehog and Mole again. Hedgehog was pushing his little handcart, which was piled high with coal. He looked tired, and his sharp little face was smeared with coal dust. Mole followed, carrying a shovel.

'You should see all my coal, Hare,' Mole called cheerfully. 'Black gold, that's what it is. Black gold! I shall soon be rich.'

'Then you'll be able to pay Hedgehog handsomely for all his hard work,' said Hare, and he winked at Hedgehog. Hedgehog grinned, and Mole looked cross.

Dormouse was curled up in a fluffy, sleepy ball in Badger's armchair. She was clutching a yellow duster in one tiny paw. Banging sounds came from the next room, where Badger was building his book-case. At each bang, Dormouse jerked almost awake, then with a tiny, whooshy snore, went back to sleep. An extra loud bang caused her to open her eyes.

'Hullo, little Dorymouse,' said Hare. 'Have you had a good winter sleep?'

'Yes, thank you, Hare. A lovely sleep,' Dormouse replied. She yawned. 'I'm afraid you will have to excuse me, Hare. I'm not properly awake yet.' And she curled herself into a snug ball, and fell alseep once more.

Badger had just finished his book-case when Hare joined him. Hare admired it, which pleased Badger so much, that he offered Hare some of his blackberry and apple wine. Each autumn, Badger raided the Orchards, and picked blackberries on his own doorstep, to make wine. Hare was delighted to be offered some, for it was very good wine, and Badger didn't often give any away.

'I'll light a fire. The evenings are still chilly, and we might as well be cosy,' Badger said. He took the coal bucket, and disappeared down the coal cellar steps. There were all kinds of steps and staircases in Badger's house, leading to bedrooms – this year's bedroom, last year's bedroom and next year's bedroom, – as well as to storerooms and spare rooms.

When he returned, Badger said: 'I haven't as much coal as I thought.'

While they sipped their wine, Hare told Badger about Mole's coal mine. 'Black gold he called it,' said Hare.

Badger grinned. 'Well, Hare, we'll go and buy some of that black gold.'

They found Mole pottering in the yard behind Mrs Mole's shop. He was delighted to learn that Badger wanted to buy some coal. 'You're my first customers,' he said. 'Perhaps you would care to see my coal mine,' he added hopefully, for he was longing to show it off to someone.

Badger replied that he had always wanted to see a coal mine. Hare said he had never given the matter much thought, but he might as well come along.

Mole put on a helmet with a miner's lamp in front, and led the way along a series of damp, dark tunnels. Hare didn't much care for underground tunnels, being an above ground animal himself; unlike Badger and Mole, who were quite at home in tunnels. He was glad when Mole said, 'Here it is. Here is my coal mine. And believe me, Badger, Hare, it is going to be a little gold mine. I shall be rich. . . .'

But Badger wasn't listening. He was staring straight ahead with a puzzled expression on his stripey face. Mole shuffled his feet uneasily. Badger scratched his head. Then growled furiously. 'Why, you stupid animal,' he snarled. 'This is no coal mine: this is *my* coal cellar! No wonder I'm short of coal. You'll put it all back, Mole, or I'll – I'll – I'll skin you, and make a moleskin footstool for Dormouse.'

He caught sight of Hare's grinning face. 'And you can stop grinning, Hare,' he snapped. 'Coal mine! Bah!'

'I shan't be rich after all,' regretted Mole, as he hurried to fetch Hedgehog's roadman's handcart, to carry the coal back to Badger's coal cellar.

Badger hurried home, muttering fiercely: 'Coal mine! I'll give him coal mine!'

And Hare – well Hare went lollopy-gallopy along The Pathway, in search of Kingfisher, to tell him about Mole's coal mine that was to have been a gold mine, but was only Badger's coal cellar after all.

Elizabeth Robinson

The Butterfly's Ball

'Come, take up your hats, and away let us haste
To the Butterfly's Ball and the Grasshopper's Feast;
The trumpeter, Gadfly, has summoned the crew,
And the revels are now only waiting for you.'

So said little Robert, and pacing along,
His merry companions came forth in a throng,
And on the smooth grass by the side of a wood,
Beneath a broad oak that for ages has stood,
Saw the children of earth and the tenants of air
For an evening's amusement together repair.

And there came the Beetle, so blind and so black,
Who carried the Emmet, his friend, on his back;
And there was the Gnat and the Dragonfly too,
With all their relations, green, orange, and blue.

And there came the moth, with his plumage of down,
And the Hornet, in jacket of yellow and brown,
Who with him the Wasp, his companion, did bring;
They promised that evening to lay by their sting.

And the sly little Dormouse crept out of his hole,
And brought to the Feast his blind brother, the Mole.
And the Snail, with his horns peeping out of his shell,
Came from a great distance – the length of an ell.

A mushroom their table, and on it was laid
A water-dock leaf, which a table-cloth made.
The viands were various, to each of their taste,
And the Bee brought her honey to crown the repast.

Then close on his haunches, so solemn and wise,
The Frog from a corner looked up to the skies;
And the squirrel, well-pleased such diversions to see,
Mounted high overhead and looked down from a tree.

Then out came a Spider, with fingers so fine,
To show his dexterity on the tight-line.
From one branch to another his cobwebs he slung,
Then quick as an arrow he darted along.

But just in the middle – oh! shocking to tell,
From his rope, in an instant, poor Harlequin fell.
Yet he touched not the ground, but with talons
    outspread,
Hung suspended in air, at the end of a thread.

Then the Grasshopper came, with a jerk and a spring,
Very long was his leg, though but short was his wing;
He took but three leaps, and was soon out of sight,
Then chirped his own praises the rest of the night.

With step so majestic, the Snail did advance,
And promised the gazers a minuet to dance:
But they all laughed so loud that he pulled in his head,
And went to his own little chamber to bed.

Then as evening gave way to the shadows of night,
Their watchman, the Glow-worm, came out with a light.
'Then home let us hasten while yet we can see,
For no watchman is waiting for you and for me.'
So said little Robert, and pacing along,
His merry companions returned in a throng.

William Roscoe

With step so majestic, the Snail did advance,
And promised the gazers a minuet to dance:

Little Jack Horner

Little Jack Horner
Sat in a corner,
Eating a Christmas pie;
He put in his thumb,
And he took out a plum,
And said, 'What a good boy am I!'

Little Miss Muffet

Little Miss Muffet
   She sat on a tuffet
      Eating of curds and whey;
There came a great spider,
Who sat down beside her,
    And frightened Miss Muffet away.

Harum Scarum

Once upon a time, in the middle of a deep wood in a cold dark castle lived a horrible magician called Harum Scarum. He was very tall and bony, with masses of floppy grey hair and a green face and green hands. He didn't just look horrible, he WAS horrible. All day long

he worked in his mysterious castle making wicked spells. Spells to give old ladies rheumatism in their knees, and babies hiccups. Spells to make schoolboys fall headlong off bicycles and all sorts of other nasty tricks.

Then one day he suddenly got very tired of making wicked spells. Harum Scarum stamped around his castle in a terrible temper. 'I AM VERY TIRED OF MAKING WICKED SPELLS,' he thundered. No one heard him because he lived completely alone in his castle, and the people who lived in the village were all too afraid to visit him. Harum Scarum felt very lonely and sad. If only he had someone to talk to, someone to live in the castle and suggest ideas for more wicked spells! How happy he would be if he had anyone to talk to. Harum Scarum thought about this problem for a long time and then he had an idea. He would go down to the village outside the wood, kidnap the first person he saw and bring him back to the cold dark castle. Harum Scarum thought about his idea for a few minutes, then he put on his hat and his cloak and set out through the wood to the village.

When the villagers saw Harum Scarum coming down the lane from the wood to the village they were terrified. They raced into their homes and bolted the doors. Shopkeepers boarded up their windows, and bus drivers left their buses in the middle of the road and ran away. By the time Harum Scarum had reached the village there was not a person to be seen anywhere.

The wicked magician clumped slowly down the deserted streets. He peered down alleyways and over hedges, hoping to find someone to kidnap. Harum Scarum felt very puzzled. Why weren't there any people about? Surely they hadn't all gone on holiday. He was just about to give up and go home, when he saw just one man standing all by himself on the pavement outside the junior school. He was the lollipop man. He was waiting for the children to come out of school so that he could see them safely across the road. He had heard that the magician was coming, but he wasn't going to leave his job just because of some silly magician. So he stayed exactly where he was.

Harum Scarum crept stealthily down the road. Then, in one quick movement, Harum Scarum had snatched up the unfortunate lollipop man and raced down the road with him. Of course, he tried to get away. He shouted and hit the magician hard with his giant lollipop stick, but it was no use. He was only a small man, and the magician was very tall and strong.

When all the children got out of school at half past three, they were puzzled to find their lollipop man was not waiting for them as usual. Most of the children thought that he must have gone to the seaside, because that was a place the lollipop man loved and often visited. So they crossed the road on their own and went home.

But some of the other children were a bit worried and decided to find out the truth.

The children went into the sweet shop opposite the school and asked Mrs Bundy if she had seen their lollipop man. 'Yes,' said Mrs Bundy, 'haven't you heard? Harum Scarum, the wicked magician from the castle in the deep wood has kidnapped him.' The children were horrified!

'What a terrible thing to happen,' said Arthur.

'Yes, it is very sad,' said Mrs Bundy. 'He was a very good lollipop man.'

'We must rescue him,' said Thomas, who was prefect of Form One, and always had good ideas.

'Yes,' agreed Elizabeth Mary, the pencil monitor.

'Yes, yes!' shouted all the other children enthusiastically. 'Come on, hurry up, let's go now before it gets dark.'

So they went.

Now nobody had been in the dark wood for years and years and it had become very untidy.

'It's very wild and overgrown,' complained Elizabeth Mary, falling over a tree root for the seventh time.

'Let's be sensible and walk in single file,' said Thomas at last. He always had the good ideas. 'It would be much

easier.' So they walked in single file with Thomas at the front because he was the bravest, and Billy Brown at the back because he wasn't the bravest. Deeper and deeper they went, holding down bramble sprays that got in the way, and stepping cautiously over the tree roots that lay in their path.

The castle was a lot further away than the children had

thought. They got very tired, and the wood got darker and darker.

'Let's go home,' wailed Billy Brown, 'I don't like this one little bit. I don't, I don't, I don't.'

'Don't be silly,' said Thomas sternly, 'we've come too far to turn back now, and anyway we must be nearly there by now.' No sooner had Thomas said that than they reached a clearing in the wood and saw a huge flight of stone steps leading up to a cold dark castle. It was Harum Scarum's castle, of course, and the children knew it.

'I think I'll stay out here,' said Billy Brown faintly. 'You can go inside and I shall wait for you here on the steps.'

'Come on in Billy Brown,' said the other children.

'Don't be a coward.' But Billy Brown shook his head firmly.

'But it's beginning to rain,' said Elizabeth Mary kindly. 'You'll get very cold and wet if you stay here.'

'I'd rather be cold and wet out here than be turned into a tin of sardines by a wicked spell in there,' shivered Billy.

'Oh, leave him then,' said Thomas impatiently. 'Let's go in.'

So they went in. It was unexpectedly easy to get into the castle, because the door wasn't locked, and as it creaked open the children crept into the hall. It was a very large hall with lots of doors on either side.

'Look for a locked door,' said Thomas in a quiet voice.

'Why a locked door?' asked Arthur. He wasn't very bright.

'Because if we're looking for the lollipop man he will be in a locked room,' explained Thomas.

The children started looking for a locked door and soon Elizabeth Mary found one. She called the others over and they drew back the heavy bolts and opened the door. Much to their disappointment the room was full of dusty books, bottles and jars. The children crowded in and looked around, but it was clear that their lollipop man was not there.

'Let's look somewhere else,' said Arthur who was growing tired of examining the little bottles and jars. None of the children wanted to stay in the castle longer than they could help. They were just about to leave the room of little bottles and jars, when the door crashed to and when the children tried to open it again they found that it was locked.

'AHA!' laughed Harum Scarum from the other side of

the door. 'I've locked you all in, you silly children. You came to rescue your lollipop man but I am not quite as stupid as you seem to think.' Then Harum Scarum ran down the hall and up the stairs laughing and clapping his hands all the way. He was going to find some more people he could kidnap in the village.

The children were feeling a bit frightened and very cross with themselves for falling into Harum Scarum's trap. They wondered how they could escape but no one could think of a good plan. Arthur suggested climbing out of the window, but the window had bars across it and couldn't be opened. Arthur was not a very bright boy. They talked for hours and hours but not even Thomas could think of an idea.

Suddenly there were footsteps in the hall and the children stopped talking and listened.

'Perhaps it is the magician, come to turn us into frogs,' said Thomas as the footsteps grew nearer and the door was unlocked.

'Or toadstools,' said Elizabeth Mary with a shudder. The door opened slowly and creakingly.

'Or double decker buses,' said Henry Smith. All the children expected Harum Scarum to come through the door, but they got a lovely surprise. Harum Scarum did not come through the door. It was Billy Brown! A very cold and a very wet Billy Brown.

He had waited on the steps for a long time and at last he had decided that something was wrong. He did not want to go back to the village for help, because the woods were now very dark and he did not want to get lost. The only thing he could do was to go into the castle and find the other children. So, although he did not like the castle a bit, he went inside and looked for a locked door. Then of course he had found the same door that Elizabeth Mary had found, and so, not quite sure what he would find on the other side, he had opened it very cautiously and had found the other children.

How pleased they were to see him! They rushed to the door, clapped Billy Brown on the back and told him how brave he was. Elizabeth Mary, the pencil monitor in school, promised to give Billy the best pencil in the box for the rest of the term. Billy Brown felt pleased and shy all at once.

'Come on,' he said, 'let's find the lollipop man.'

Suddenly the lollipop man was not difficult to find. This was because he had heard the children and was shouting and yelling things like, 'UNLOCK THIS DOOR IMMEDIATELY. LET ME OUT OF THIS BROOM CUPBOARD, AT ONCE. I'M TOO HOT AND VERY CROSS.'

Thomas looked around for a broom cupboard and when he had found it he unlocked the door and let out a very bewildered lollipop man. He looked, as he had said, too hot, and very cross.

Of course he was very surprised to see the children, but there was no time to talk as the children wanted to get home as quickly as possible. Outside it was raining hard but the lollipop man knew a short cut home and he walked in front, beating down nettles and weeds with his giant lollipop stick.

When all the children were safely back home their mothers made them have baths because they were all very dirty. Then as the next day was a Saturday, the lollipop man took them all to the seaside as a reward. The children were very pleased because the seaside was one of their favourite places.

As for Harum Scarum, he was so ashamed that he had let a few children outwit him that he gave up being horrible and wicked. He threw away all his dusty spell books and strange bottles and jars and took up cookery instead. He's been a lot happier since. It's not much fun, he decided, being a nasty horrible magician that nobody liked. Instead, every now and then he takes some cakes he has made and gives them to the villagers. At first they were too frightened to eat them, but when they saw that cats and dogs who ate them came to no harm they began to eat them and now Harum Scarum is a great favourite with them, especially at Christmas time when he holds a party in his castle.

Jane Barry

Ding, Dong, Bell

Ding, dong, bell
Pussy's in the well.
Who put her in?
Little Tommy Green.
Who pulled her out?
Little Tommy Trout.
What a naughty boy was that,
To try and drown poor Pussy Cat.

Mary, Mary, Quite Contrary

Mary, Mary, quite contrary,
How does your garden grow?
Silver bells and cockle-shells,
And pretty maids all in a row.

The Pig-Tale

There was a Pig that sat alone
   Beside a ruined Pump:
By day and night he made his moan –
It would have stirred a heart of stone
To see him wring his hoofs and groan,
   Because he could not jump.

A certain Camel heard him shout –
   A Camel with a hump.
'Oh, is it Grief, or is it Gout?
What is this bellowing about?'
That Pig replied, with quivering snout,
   'Because I cannot jump!'

That Camel scanned him, dreamy-eyed.
   'Methinks you are too plump.
I never knew a Pig so wide –
That wobbled so from side to side –
Who could, however, much he tried,
   Do such a thing as *jump*!

'Yet mark those trees, two miles away,
   All clustered in a clump:
If you could trot there twice a day,
Nor ever pause for rest or play,
In the far future – who can say? –
   You may be fit to jump.'

That Camel passed, and left him there
   Beside the ruined Pump.

Oh, horrid was that Pig's despair!
His shrieks of anguish filled the air.
He wrung his hoofs, he rent his hair,
  Because he could not jump.

There was a Frog that wandered by –
  A sleek and shining lump:
Inspected him with fishy eye,
And said: 'O Pig, what makes you cry?'
And bitter was that Pig's reply,
  'Because I cannot jump!'

That Frog he grinned a grin of glee,
  And hit his chest a thump.
'O Pig,' he said, 'be ruled by me,
And you shall see what you shall see.
This minute, for a trifling fee,
  I'll teach you how to jump!

'You may be faint from many a fall,
  And bruised by many a bump:
But if you persevere through all,
And practise first on something small,
Concluding with a ten-foot wall,
  You'll find that you *can* jump!'

That Pig looked up with joyful start:
  'Oh, Frog, you *are* a trump!
Your words have healed my inward smart -
Come, name your fee and do your part:
Bring comfort to a broken heart,
  By teaching me to jump!'

'My fee shall be a mutton-chop,
    My goal this ruined Pump.
Observe with what an airy flop
I plant myself upon the top!
Now bend your knees and take a hop,
    For that's the way to jump!'

Up rose that Pig, and rushed, full whack,
    Against the ruined Pump:
Rolled over like an empty sack,
And settled down upon his back,
While all his bones at once went 'Crack!'
    It was a fatal jump.

That Camel passed, as day grew dim
    Around the ruined Pump.
'O broken heart! O broken limb!
It needs,' that Camel said to him,
'Something more fairy-like and slim,
    To execute a jump!'

That Pig lay still as any stone,
    And could not stir a stump:
Nor ever, if the truth were known,
Was he again observed to moan,
Nor ever wring his hoofs and groan,
    Because he could not jump.

That Frog made no remark, for he
    Was dismal as a dump:
He knew the consequence must be
That he would never get his fee –
And still he sits, in miserie,
    Upon that ruined Pump!

Lewis Carroll

Mice

I think mice
Are rather nice.

> Their tails are long,
> Their faces small,
> They haven't any
> Chins at all.
> Their ears are pink,
> Their teeth are white,
> They run about
> The house at night.
> They nibble things
> They shouldn't touch
> And no one seems
> To like them much.

But I think mice
Are nice.

Rose Fyleman

Tim Rabbit and the Scissors

One day Tim Rabbit found a pair of scissors lying on the common. They had been dropped by somebody's mother, when she sat darning somebody's socks. Tim saw them shining in the grass, so he crept up very softly, just in case they might spring at him. Nearer and nearer he crept, but the scissors did not move, so he touched them with his whiskers, very gently, just in case they might bite him. He took a sniff at them, but nothing happened. Then he licked them, boldly, and, as the scissors were closed, he wasn't hurt. He admired the bright glitter of the steel, so he picked them up and carried them carefully home.

'Oh!' cried Mrs Rabbit, when he dragged them into the kitchen. 'Oh! Whatever's that shiny thing? A snake? Put it down, Tim!'

'It's a something I've found in the grass,' said Tim, proudly, 'It's quite tame.'

Mrs Rabbit examined the scissors, twisting and turning them, until she found that they opened and shut. She wisely put them on the table.

'We'll wait till your father comes home,' said she. 'He's gone to a meeting about the lateness of the swallows this year, but he said he wouldn't be long.'

'What have we here?' exclaimed Mr Rabbit when he returned.

'It's something Tim found,' said Mrs Rabbit, looking proudly at her son, and Tim held up his head and put his paws behind his back, just as his father did at a public meeting. Mr Rabbit opened the scissors and felt the sharp edges.

74

'Why! They're shears!' he cried, excitedly. 'They will trim the cowslip banks and cut the hay ready for the haystacks, when we gather our provender in the autumn.'

'Wait a minute!' he continued, snipping and snapping in the air. 'Wait a minute. I'll show you.' He ran out, carrying the scissors under his arm. In a few moments he came back with a neat bundle of grass, tied in a little sheaf.

'We can eat this in the peace and safety of our own house, by our own fireside, instead of sitting in the cold open fields,' said he. 'This is a wonderful thing you have found, Tim.'

Tim smiled happily, and asked, 'Will it cut other things, Father?'

'Yes, anything you like. Lettuces, lavender, dandelions, daisies, butter, and buttercups,' answered Mr Rabbit, but he put the scissors safely out of reach on a high shelf before he had his supper.

The next day, when his parents had gone to visit a neighbour, young Tim climbed on a stool and lifted down the bright scissors. Then he began to cut 'anything'.

First he snipped his little sheep's-wool blanket into bits, and then he snipped the leafy tablecloth into shreds. Next he cut into strips the blue window curtains which his mother had embroidered with gossamer threads, and then he spoilt the tiny roller-towel which hung behind the door. He turned his attention on himself, and trimmed his whiskers till nothing was left. Finally he started to cut off his fur. How delightful it was to see it drop in a flood of soft brown on the kitchen floor! How silky it was! He didn't know he had so much, and he clipped and clipped, twisting his neck and screwing round to the back, till the floor was covered with a furry fleece.

He felt so free and gay, so cool and happy, that he put the scissors away and danced lightly out of the room and on to the common like a dandelion-clock or a thistle-down.

Mrs Rabbit met him as she returned with her basket full of lettuces and little cabbage-plants, given to her by the kind neighbour, who had a garden near the village. She nearly fainted when she saw the strange white dancing little figure.

'Oh! Oh! Oh!' she shrieked, 'Whatever's this?'

'Mother, it's me,' laughed Tim, leaping round her like a newly-shorn lamb.

'No, it's not my Tim,' she cried sadly. 'My Tim is a fat fluffy little rabbit. You are a white rat, escaped from a menagerie. Go away.'

'Mother, it *is* me!' persisted Tim. 'It's Tim, your own Timothy Rabbit.' He danced and leaped over the basket which Mrs Rabbit had dropped on the ground.

'No! No! Go away!' she exclaimed, running into her house and shutting the door.

Tim flopped on the doorstep. One big tear rolled down his cheek and splashed on the grass. Then another and another followed in a stream.

'It *is* me,' he sobbed, with his nose against the crack of the door.

Inside the house Mrs Rabbit was gathering up the fur.

'It must have been Tim after all,' she sighed. 'This is his pretty hair. Oh, deary, deary me! Whatever shall I do?'

She opened the door. Tim popped his nose inside and sneezed.

'A-tishoo! A-tishoo! I'm so cold. A-tishoo! I won't do it again. I will be good,' he sniffed.

'Come in, young rabbit,' said Mrs Rabbit, severely. 'Get into bed at once, while I make a dose of hot camomile tea.'

But when Tim crept into bed there was no blanket. Poor Mrs Rabbit covered him with her own patchwork quilt, and then she gave him the hot posset.

'Now you must stay here till your fur grows again,' said she, and Tim lay underneath the red and blue patches of the bed-cover, thinking of the fun on the common, the leaping and galloping and turning somersaults of the little rabbits of the burrows, and he would not be there to join in.

Mr Rabbit was thoroughly shocked when he came home and saw his son, but he was a rabbit of ingenuity. He went out at once to borrow a spinning-wheel from an ancient rabbit who made coats to wrap Baby-Buntings in.

All day Mrs Rabbit wove the bits of fur, to make a little brown coat to keep Tim warm. When all the hairs were used up she pinned it round Tim with a couple of tiny sharp thorns from her pin-cushion.

'There you are, dressed again in your own fur,' said she, and she put a stitch here and there to make it fit.

How all the animals laughed when Tim ran out on the common, with his little white legs peeping out from the bottom of the funny short coat! How ashamed he was of his whiskerless face!

'Baa! Baa! White sheep! Have you any wool?' mocked his enemies the magpies, when he ran near the wall where they perched. But Tim's fur soon grew again, and then his troubles were over.

He hung his little coat on a gorse-bush for the chaffinches to take for their nests, and very glad they were to get it, too. As for the scissors, they are still lying on the high shelf, and you may see them if you peep down the rabbit hole on the edge of the common, where Tim Rabbit lives.

Alison Uttley

Doctor Foster

Doctor Foster went to Glo'ster,
In a shower of rain;
He stepped in a puddle,
   up to the middle,
And never went there again.

Calico Pie

I

Calico Pie,
The little Birds fly
Down to the calico tree,
Their wings were blue,
And they sang 'Tilly-loo!'
Till away they flew –
And they never came back to me!
They never came back!
They never came back!
They never came back to me!

Calico Jam,
The little Fish swam
Over the syllabub sea,
He took off his hat,
To the Sole and the Sprat,
And the Willeby-wat –

But he never came back to me!
He never came back!
He never came back!
He never came back to me!

III

Calico Ban,
The little Mice ran,
To be ready in time for tea,
Flippity flup,
They drank it all up,
And danced in the cup –

But they never came back to me!
   They never came back!
   They never came back!
They never came back to me!

      IV
   Calico Drum,
   The Grasshoppers come,
The Butterfly, Beetle, and Bee,
   Over the ground,
   Around and round,
   With a hop and a bound –

But they never came back!
   They never came back!
   They never came back!
They never came back to me!

Edward Lear

Limericks by Edward Lear

There was an Old Person of Ware,
Who rode on the back of a Bear;
    When they ask'd 'Does it trot?'
    He said: 'Certainly not!
He's a Moppsikon Floppsikon Bear!'

There was a Young Person of Janina,
Whose uncle was always a-fanning her;
    When he fanned off her head,
    She smiled sweetly and said:
'You propitious Old Person of Janina!'

There was an Old Man of West Dumpet,
Who possessed a large Nose like a Trumpet;
    When he blew it aloud,
    It astonished the crowd,
And was heard through the whole of West Dumpet.

There was an Old Man of Port Grigor,
Whose actions were noted for vigour;
    He stood on his head,
    Till his waistcoat turned red,
That eclectic Old Man of Port Grigor.

There was an Old Man of Ancona,
Who found a small Dog with no Owner,
   Which he took up and down
   All the streets of the town;
That anxious Old Man of Ancona.

There was an Old Person of Cassel,
Whose Nose finished off in a Tassel;
   But they call'd out: 'Oh well! –
   Don't it look like a bell!'
Which perplexed that Old Person of Cassel.

There was an Old Man of Cashmere,
Whose movements were scroobious and queer;
    Being slender and tall,
    He looked over a wall,
And perceived two fat Ducks of Cashmere.

There was an Old Person of Wilts,
Who constantly walked upon Stilts;
    He wreathed them with lilies
    And daffy-down-dillies,
That elegant Person of Wilts.

There was an Old Man of Spithead,
Who opened the window and said:
  'Fil-jomble, fil-jumble,
  Fil-rumble-come-tumble!'
That doubtful Old Man of Spithead.

There was an Old Man who said: 'How
Shall I flee from that horrible cow?
  I will sit on this stile,
  And continue to smile,
Which may soften the heart of that cow.'

There was an Old Man of the Dargle,
Who purchased six barrels of Gargle;
 For he said: 'I'll sit still,
 And will roll them down hill,
For the fish in the depths of the Dargle.'

There was an Old Person of Slough,
Who danced at the end of a Bough;
 But they said: 'If you sneeze,
 You might damage the trees,
You imprudent Old Person of Slough.'

There was an Old Person of Ewell,
Who chiefly subsisted on gruel;
 But to make it more nice
 He inserted some mice,
Which refreshed that Old Person of Ewell.

There was an Old Man, who when little
Fell casually into a Kettle;
 But, growing too stout,
 He could never get out,
So he passed all his life in that Kettle.

There was an Old man of Thermopylae,
Who never did anything properly;
    But they said: 'If you choose
    To boil Eggs in your Shoes,
You shall never remain in Thermopylae.'

There was an Old Person of Pinner,
As thin as a lath, if not thinner;
    They dressed him in white,
    And roll'd him up tight,
That elastic Old Person of Pinner.

There was an Old Man of The Hague,
Whose ideas were excessively vague;
    He built a balloon
    To examine the moon,
That deluded Old Man of The Hague.

There was an Old Man of the coast,
Who placidly sat on a post;
    But when it was cold
    He relinquished his hold
And called for some hot buttered toast.

There was an Old Man who said: 'Hush!
I perceive a young bird in this bush!'
    When they said 'Is it small?'
    He replied: 'Not at all!
It is four times as big as the bush!'

There was an Old Man of the West,
Who never could get any rest;
    So they set him to spin
    On his nose and his chin,
Which cured that Old Man of the West.

Henry Duck

Mr and Mrs Duck lived by the edge of a bright blue pond in the middle of a bright green meadow, and they couldn't think of any place where they would rather have been.

'Ooh!' said Mrs Duck one morning.

'What's the matter?' asked Mr Duck, alarmed.

'Nothing the matter dear,' said Mrs Duck, 'I've just laid two eggs.'

'So you have!' exclaimed Mr Duck. 'Well done mother!'

The two ducks took turns to sit on the eggs, because Mr Duck insisted that a GOOD father should share the baby-sitting ... well, the egg-sitting anyway. After several weeks, when the sun was very hot, one of the eggs cracked open and out rolled a baby duckling.

'Aaaah! isn't he sweet?' gasped Mrs Duck.

'Extraordinarily so!' agreed Mr Duck.

And they called him Gilbert.

Gilbert waddled into the pond and straightaway began to swim.

Just then, the other egg cracked open and out rolled the second duckling.

'Oh, come and look!' cried Mrs Duck, 'Isn't HE sweet?'

'A WONDERFUL family we have!' exclaimed Mr Duck.

And they called him Henry.

But Henry did NOT waddle down to the pond, and he did NOT straightaway begin to swim, – instead, he lay on the bank with his wings behind his head and kept his eyes shut.

'Curious that,' said Mr Duck. 'I mean, look at Gilbert out there – paddling around as if he'd been doing it all his life.'

'He HAS been doing it all his life,' put in Mrs Duck, a little timidly.

Mr Duck looked cross at this so Mrs Duck said, 'I think our Henry is thinking. THAT'S what he's doing– he's THINKING.'

'AH ... well then ... that's different isn't it!' Mr Duck puffed out his chest proudly. 'Of course, I don't

mind him just lying there like that if he's THINKING.'

Next morning, bright and early, Henry leapt up and shouted, 'I've been thinking!'

'Told you so didn't I ?' whispered Mrs Duck, nudging her husband.

'And what have you been thinking about my boy ?' asked Mr Duck.

'. . . that the world couldn't possibly end at the top of that hill. There must be more of it.'

'MORE of it!' exclaimed Mr Duck, 'more world than the blue pond and the green meadow ? Of course there isn't – and here's me thinking I'd reared a clever, thinking duck!'

'Well, I don't believe it,' said Henry. And before anyone could stop him he had waddled off.

What a shocking thing.

When Henry reached the top of the hill he saw at once that he had indeed been right: there was LOTS more world. There were fields and hedges and rivers and woods, – and twisting its way between them all was a sandy path.

Joyfully, Henry ran down the other side of the hill to where the sandy path had its beginnings. At once, he met a caterpillar who was munching his way through a field of lettuce. When the caterpillar saw Henry he said –

'Oh my goodness! You are too young to be out on your own. Go home before something terrible happens to you!'

'I'll go home when I've seen the world,' said Henry, and he ran off thinking the caterpillar knew nothing.

In a short while, he met a field mouse, nibbling nuts under a hazelnut tree. When the field mouse saw Henry she said –

'Oh dearie dearie me! such a small duckling, his feathers hardly dry – go home before something terrible happens to you.'

'I'll go home when I've seen the world,' said Henry, and he hurried on thinking the field mouse was making a fuss about nothing.

Not very much further on, he came across a large rabbit, crunching carrots. When the rabbit saw Henry he gasped, 'My whiskers! What's a young 'un like you doing out this far? Go home before something terrible happens to you.'

'I'll go home when I've seen the world,' said Henry and he ran on faster than ever, hoping not to meet any more tiresome creatures until he'd finished looking round the world.

He ran for a long time until he came to the edge of a dark silent wood. Henry didn't like the wood much. It was creepy woohy. In the middle of the horrible darkness lurked a fox. The fox was red with pointed ears, a pointed nose, and a long bushy tail. Its teeth were like the edges of two saws.

'I'm not going home until I've seen the world, so don't scold me,' said Henry to the fox.

'Scold you? Tell you to go home? Nothing was further from my mind,' said the fox.

'It wasn't?' Henry was surprised.

'Certainly not,' said the fox. 'It is very obvious to me that you are a clever duck and I have been looking far and wide for such a creature with whom to tour the world.'

'You have?' said Henry, even more surprised.

'Certainly I have. But listen,' said the fox, putting his mouth to Henry's ear, 'we should have dinner before we go – give us strength you know, sustain us on the journey.'

So Henry went home with the fox and helped to prepare the dinner. He peeled potatoes, shelled peas, mixed stuffing, and stirred the gravy. When everything was ready the fox and the duck sat down.

'Oh dear,' said the fox, 'I see that you cannot reach. Never mind about good manners – sit on the table.'

Henry climbed on to the table, but the plate was too large. Still he could not reach.

'My poor fellow!' said the fox, 'you seem to be having extraordinary difficulty reaching your meal. I would not blame you one bit if you were to actually sit on the plate!'

Henry did so. Fortunately for him, he sat on a hot potato for at that very moment the fox tried to stab the duckling with his knife and fork meaning to eat him.

'Quack!' yelled Henry, leaping high into the air.

'Bother!' said the fox, seeing his 'dinner' dashing off with gravy on its feathers.

Henry ran all the way home. He reached the hill and from the top of it he could see the bright blue pond and the bright green field – HIS world.

'Look,' said Mrs Duck, 'isn't that our Henry up at the top of the hill?' Mr Duck shaded his eyes. 'I do believe it is, Mother.'

'Well, don't be harsh with him,' begged his wife.

'As if I would!' exclaimed Mr Duck, 'just as if I would!'

Henry came home, and straightaway he swam out to an island in the middle of the bright blue pond. Gilbert grew up to be a fine duck and went on world cruises at least once a year, but Henry never wanted to leave his safe little island.

Margaret Stuart Barry

The Old Gumbie Cat

I have a Gumbie Cat in mind, her name is Jennyanydots;
Her coat is of the tabby kind, with tiger stripes and
    leopard spots.
All days she sits upon the stair or on the steps or on the
    mat:
She sits and sits and sits – and that's what makes a
    Gumbie Cat!

But when the day's hustle and bustle is done,
Then the Gumbie Cat's work is but hardly begun.
And when all the family's in bed and asleep,
She tucks up her skirts to the basement to creep.
She is deeply concerned with the ways of the mice –
Their behaviour's not good and their manners not
    nice;
So when she has got them lined up on the matting,
She teaches them music, crocheting and tatting.

I have a Gumbie Cat in mind, her name is Jennyanydots;
Her equal would be hard to find, she likes the warm and
    sunny spots.
All day she sits beside the hearth or on the bed or on my
    hat:
She sits and sits and sits and sits – and that's what makes
    a Gumbie Cat!

But when the day's hustle and bustle is done,
Then the Gumbie Cat's work is but hardly begun.
As she finds that the mice will not ever keep quiet.
She is sure it is due to irregular diet;
And believing that nothing is done without trying,
She sets right to work with her baking and frying.
She makes them a mouse-cake of bread and dried peas,
And a *beautiful* fry of lean bacon and cheese.

I have a Gumbie Cat in mind, her name is Jennyanydots;
The curtain-cord she likes to wind, and tie it into sailor-
  knots.
She sits upon the window-sill, or anything that's smooth
  and flat:
She sits and sits and sits and sits – and that's what makes
  a Gumbie Cat!

But when the day's hustle and bustle is done,
Then the Gumbie Cat's work is but hardly begun.
She thinks that the cockroaches just need employment
To prevent them from idle and wanton destroyment.
So she's formed, from that lot of disorderly louts
A troop of well-disciplined helpful boy-scouts,
With a purpose in life and a good deed to do –
And she's even created a Beetles' Tattoo.

So for Old Gumbie Cats let us now give three cheers
On whom well-ordered households depend, it appears.

T. S. Eliot

Miranda

Miranda is a tiny mouse
Smooth and quick and pretty
She lives at the bottom of a big big house
Right in the middle of the city

    And there in a hole at the bottom of the stairs
    The mice all hide from the day's affairs
    For who goes out by day, who dares?
    In the house in the middle of the city?

But night is the time the mice come out
Listen! Hard, and harder!
Shuffle and scuffle and snuffle and snout!
Scuffing about in the larder!

    And there in the night are fresh green peas
    And cakes and crumbs and rind of cheese
    And why would a mouse want more than these
    At night in the downstair larder?

O what would make a tiny mouse,
Smooth and quick and pretty,
Climb on the stairs of the big big house
Right in the middle of the city?

    Away from the cheese and the cakes and the bread
    Why should a mouse climb up instead
    To the top of the stair, to the topmost tread
    In the house in the middle of the city?

Up she goes through the attic door
In by a chink that's handy
Over the moonlit mouldering floor
Up on a box goes Mandy

And there on the books left open wide
The quick little paws go slither and slide
With eyes to look and a nose to guide –
And the words all speak to Mandy

And all the time and all the night
While other mice are feeding
Miranda's there in the moonlight bright
Reading! Reading! Reading!

Away from the cakes and the bread and the cheese
And the beef and the ham and the fresh green
    peas
Miranda knows more words than these
By reading, reading, reading!

O who has ever seen or heard
A mouse so quick and clever?
Miranda always knows the word
Miranda falters never!

One night by the hole at the foot of the stair
She saw some cheese on a little board there
And the words 'Mouse Trap' – she cried
    'Beware!
O touch it not! No, never!'

Miranda is a mighty mouse
Smooth and small and pretty
She lives at the bottom of a big big house
Right in the middle of the city

And there in a hole at the bottom of the stairs
She's QUEEN OF THE MICE AND MOUSE
    AFFAIRS
For she knows all the words and the why's and the
    where's
And the what's in the middle of the city.

Richard Parker

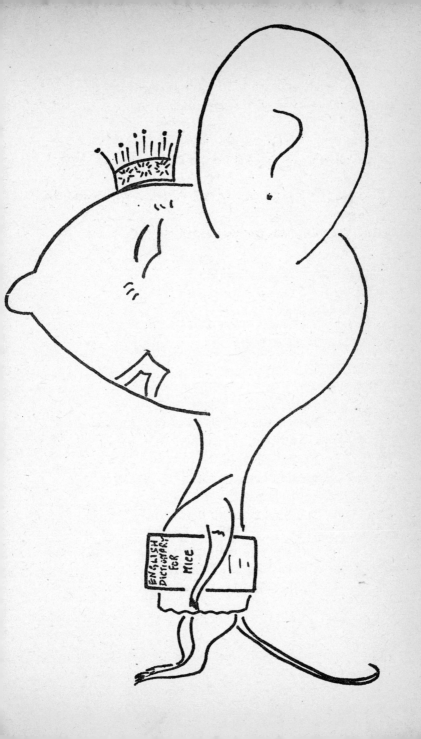

The Courtship of the
Yonghy-Bonghy-Bò

I

On the Coast of Coromandel
  Where the early pumpkins blow,
    In the middle of the woods
  Lived the Yonghy-Bonghy-Bò.
Two old chairs, and half a candle –
One old jug without a handle –
    These were all his worldly goods:
    In the middle of the woods,
    These were all the worldly goods,
  Of the Yonghy-Bonghy-Bò,
  Of the Yonghy-Bonghy-Bò.

II

Once, among the Bong-trees walking
　　Where the early pumpkins blow,
　　　To a little heap of stones
　　Came the Yonghy-Bonghy-Bò.
There he heard a Lady talking,
To some milk-white Hens of Dorking –
　　　' 'Tis the Lady Jingly Jones!
　　　On that little heap of stones
　　　Sits the Lady Jingly Jones!'
　　Said the Yonghy-Bonghy-Bò,
　　Said the Yonghy-Bonghy-Bò.

III

'Lady Jingly! Lady Jingly!
　　Sitting where the pumpkins blow,
　　　Will you come and be my wife?'
　　Said the Yonghy-Bonghy-Bò.
'I am tired of living singly –
On this coast so wild and shingly –
　　　I'm a-weary of my life;
　　　If you'll come and be my wife,
　　　Quite serene would be my life!'
　　Said the Yonghy-Bonghy-Bò,
　　Said the Yonghy-Bonghy-Bò.

IV

'On this Coast of Coromandel,
 Shrimps and watercresses grow,
  Prawns are plentiful and cheap,'
 Said the Yonghy-Bonghy-Bò.
'You shall have my chairs and candle,
And my jug without a handle! –
  Gaze upon the rolling deep
  (Fish is plentiful and cheap);
  As the sea, my love is deep!'
 Said the Yonghy-Bonghy-Bò,
 Said the Yonghy-Bonghy-Bò.

V

Lady Jingly answered sadly,
 And her tears began to flow –
  'Your proposal comes too late,
 Mr Yonghy-Bonghy-Bò!
I would be your wife most gladly!'
(Here she twirled her fingers madly)
  'But in England I've a mate!
  Yes! you've asked me far too late,
  For in England I've a mate,
 Mr Yonghy-Bonghy-Bò!
 Mr Yonghy-Bonghy-Bò!

VI

'Mr Jones – (his name is Handel –
　　Handel Jones, Esquire, & Co.)
　　　Dorking fowls delights to send,
　　Mr Yonghy-Bonghy-Bò!
Keep, oh! keep your chairs and candle,
And your jug without a handle –
　　　I can merely be your friend!
　　　– Should my Jones more Dorkings send,
　　　I will give you three, my friend!
　　Mr Yonghy-Bonghy-Bò!
　　Mr Yonghy-Bonghy-Bò!

VII

'Though you've such a tiny body,
　　And your head so large doth grow –
　　　Though your hat may blow away,
　　Mr Yonghy-Bonghy-Bò!
Though you're such a Hoddy-Doddy –
Yet I wish that I could modi-
　　　fy the words I needs must say!
　　　Will you please to go away?
　　　That is all I have to say –
　　Mr Yonghy-Bonghy-Bò!
　　Mr Yonghy-Bonghy-Bò!'

Down the slippery slopes of Myrtle,
  Where the early pumpkins blow,
    To the calm and silent sea
    Fled the Yonghy-Bonghy-Bò.
There, beyond the Bay of Gurtle,
Lay a large and lively Turtle –

'You're the Cove,' he said, 'for me;
  On your back beyond the sea,
    Turtle, you shall carry me!'
Said the Yonghy-Bonghy-Bò,
Said the Yonghy-Bonghy-Bò.

IX

Through the silent-roaring ocean
  Did the Turtle swiftly go;
    Holding fast upon his shell
  Rode the Yonghy-Bonghy-Bò.
With a sad primeval motion
Towards the sunset isles of Boshen
    Still the Turtle bore him well.
    Holding fast upon his shell,
    'Lady Jingly Jones, farewell!'
  Sang the Yonghy-Bonghy-Bò,
  Sang the Yonghy-Bonghy-Bò.

X

From the Coast of Coromandel,
  Did that Lady never go;
    On the heap of stones she mourns
  For the Yonghy-Bonghy-Bò.
On the Coast of Coromandel,
In his jug without a handle,
    Still she weeps, and daily moans,
    On that little heap of stones
    To her Dorking Hens she moans,
  For the Yonghy-Bonghy-Bò,
  For the Yonghy-Bonghy-Bò.

Edward Lear

The Fisherman

I met a little fisherman
 Dressed in a spotted coat.
He told me he was off to fish
 Out in a rubber boat.

Around his waist he wore a belt
 Of rainbow blue and pink
To keep him floating safely
 If his little boat should sink.

He asked me if I'd like to go
 And fish with him that night.
'My boat is very small,' he said,
 'And we must squash in tight.'

'You'll have to trust me, sir,' he said,
 'Out in the deep blue sea.'
'O, I shall trust you, sir,' I said,
 'And happy I shall be.'

He led me to a whisp'ring tree
 Whereto his boat was tied;
He held the rope while I got in,
 And sat me down inside.

We sailed away into the night
 And left the whisp'ring tree
Whisp'ring a farewell whisper to
 My fisherman and me.

I saw the full moon's yellow face
    Ride up into the sky,
And all its light upon the sea
    Like buttercups did lie.

The bright stars twinkled all around,
    So near they seemed to be,
They danced like shining butterflies
    Around my friend and me.

We never caught a fish that night,
    But, O! a fish caught me,
And carried me away and down
    Into the cold, dark sea.

He swam with me into a cave,
    And I began to cry,
When suddenly I saw a light
    And heard a voice close by.

The big fish turned and swam away –
    He went and left me free,
And I was in a garden fair,
    Under a bonbon tree.

And lovely things there were to eat,
    And lovely things to see,
And lovely flowers there were to smell
    Beneath the bonbon tree.

But where is gone my fisherman,
    All in his spotted coat?
And where is gone his whisp'ring tree?
    And where his rubber boat?
                                Francis Mott

The Hippopotamus Song

A bold Hippopotamus was standing one day
On the banks of the cool Shalimar.
He gazed at the bottom as it peacefully lay
By the light of the evening star.
Away on the hill top sat combing her hair
His fair Hippopotamine maid.
The Hippopotamus
Was no ignoramus
And sang her this sweet serenade.
   Mud! Mud!
   Glorious Mud!
   Nothing quite like it for cooling the blood.
   So, follow me, follow, down to the hollow,
   And there let us wallow in glorious mud.

The fair Hippopotamus he aimed to entice
From her seat on the hill top above
As she hadn't got a ma to give her advice
Came tiptoeing down to her love.
Like thunder the forest re-echoed the sound
Of the song that they sang as they met
His inamorata
Adjusted her garter
And lifted her voice in duet.
  Mud! Mud!
  Glorious mud!
  Nothing quite like it for cooling the blood.
  So, follow me, follow, down to the hollow,
  And there let us wallow in glorious mud.

Now more Hippopotami began to convene
On the banks of that river so wide.
I wonder now what am I to say of the scene
That ensued by the Shalimar side.
They dived all at once with an ear-splitting splosh,
Then rose to the surface again,
A regular army
Of Hippopotami
All singing this haunting refrain.
  Mud! Mud!
  Glorious mud!
  Nothing quite like it for cooling the blood.
  So follow me, follow, down to the hollow,
  And there let us wallow in glorious mud!

Michael Flanders

Halfway Down

Halfway down the stairs
Is a stair
Where I sit.
There isn't any
Other stair
Quite like
It.
I'm not at the bottom,
I'm not at the top;
So this is the stair
Where
I always
Stop.

Halfway up the stairs
Isn't up,
And isn't down.
It isn't in the nursery,
It isn't in the town.
And all sorts of funny thoughts
Run round my head:
'It isn't really
Anywhere!
It's somewhere else
Instead!'

A. A. Milne

The Bobtail Bunns go to Town

At Hutch End one morning, five rabbits climbed aboard the London-bound bus: Grandma Bunn, wearing her best straw hat with buttercups on it, and carrying an umbrella that was almost as tall as she was; plump Mummy Bunn, carrying a munch-bag filled with carrots for the journey; Violet and Hyacinth the Twins; and Daddy Bunn, wearing his best brown waistcoat and his usual worried expression. They were the Bobtail Bunns, off to London on holiday.

Inside the bus were Mr Octavious Browne – with an E, and a Disagreeable Bus Conductor.

Grandma Bunn inclined her head. 'Good morning,' she said.

'Good morning,' replied Mr Browne politely.

Mummy Bunn smiled her company smile. 'Nice,' she said. 'For the time of year.'

'Very nice,' agreed Mr Browne.

Daddy Bunn smiled nervously. 'I fear we shall see rain before long,' he said.

'Before dark,' returned the agreeable Mr Browne.

The Disagreeable Bus Conductor didn't say anything at all.

Berr-um! Berr-um! said the bus, as it rattled on its way.

The agreeable Mr Browne looked at his newspaper.

The Disagreeable Bus Conductor looked at the Bobtail Bunns. 'Rabbits! nice fat rabbits,' he said to himself. 'Hm, hm . . .' and he began to think of one of his favourite dishes – rabbit pie: succulent, golden-crusted, steam-rising-from-it, *delicious* rabbit pie.

118

Grandma Bunn, who was sensitive to such thoughts, quivered with rage. 'I'll give him rabbit pie!' she vowed.

At the next stop the Disagreeable Bus Conductor rang the bell, and the bus stopped. With a polite 'Good-day' Mr Browne got off. The Disagreeable Bus Conductor got off too, to fetch Mr Browne's luggage from the boot at the back of the bus.

Grandma Bunn prodded the bell with the sharp end of her umbrella, and the bus went rattling on its way. The Disagreeable Bus Conductor ran behind it, waving and shouting, and pulling funny, furious faces.

'Poor Bus Conductor!' giggled Violet and Hyacinth the Twins.

'Fiddlesticks!' snapped Grandma Bunn. 'He had to be taught a lesson. He was thinking about *you-know-what*.'

'That was asking for trouble,' said Mummy Bunn, taking a carrot from her munch-bag.

'There'll be more trouble before we're done,' said Daddy Bunn. 'We should have stayed at home.'

'Tush, Reginald!' snapped Grandma Bunn. 'You worry too much.'

Berr-um! Berr-um! said the bus, as it rattled on its way. When it reached London Bridge Grandma Bunn prodded the bell with the sharp end of her umbrella. The bus stopped, and the Bobtail Bunns got off. As there was no one left to ring the bell again, the driver went to sleep until he was wakened by the Disagreeable Bus Conductor, who arrived panting and very angry after running for half an hour.

The Bobtail Bunns walked the streets of London searching for somewhere to live: Grandma Bunn, wearing her best straw hat with buttercups on it, and carrying an umbrella that was almost as tall as she was; plump Mummy Bunn, carrying a munch-bag with nothing left in it; Violet and Hyacinth the Twins; and Daddy Bunn, wearing his best brown waistcoat and his usual worried expression.

The people of London stared and nudged and whispered, but the Bobtail Bunns took no notice. Looking neither to right nor left, they went on their way until they came to a large house, with a very smart garden at the back of it, and a soldier guarding the front of it.

'This will do nicely,' said Grandma Bunn. She led the way across a courtyard, along a paved path, into the garden of Buckingham Palace. There the Bobtail Bunns made themselves at home among the Michaelmas daisies. At dusk they squeezed through a trellis into the vegetable garden beyond, where they feasted royally on:

> turnips and parsnips;
> corncobs and carrots;
> peas and asparagus;
> celery, chicory and young green beans.

And Mummy Bunn refilled her munch-bag.

Next morning three gardeners came.

'There are rabbits in the herbaceous border,' said the First Gardener.

'They have ravaged the vegetable garden,' said the Second Gardener.

'They must be taken care of,' said the Forbidding Third Gardener.

'Yes,' agreed the other two. 'They'll have to be taken care of.'

The First and Second, and the Forbidding Third

Gardener looked at one another, and they knew that they were all thinking of the same thing – rabbit stew: rich, savoury, dumplings-bobbing-in-it, *delicious* rabbit stew.

Under the Michaelmas daisies Grandma Bunn, who was sensitive to such thoughts, quivered with rage. 'I'll give them rabbit stew!' she vowed.

A footman came into the garden. He said that one of the Royal Princesses wished to inspect the roses. When she arrived, the three Gardeners must stand up straight in a row, take one step forward, and bow.

The Three Gardeners nodded, and practised taking-one-step-forward-and-bowing until the Royal Princess arrived. Then they stood up straight in a row, took one step forward – and fell flat on their faces. Grandma Bunn had tied their shoelaces together.

'Poor gardeners!' giggled Violet and Hyacinth the Twins.

'Fiddlesticks!' snapped Grandma Bunn. 'They had to be taught a lesson. They were thinking of *you-know-what*.'

'That was asking for trouble,' said Mummy Bunn. And she went to refill her munch-bag.

'I fear we haven't heard the last of this,' said Daddy Bunn nervously. 'We should have stayed at home.'

'Tush, Reginald!' snapped Grandma Bunn. 'You worry too much. I'm going shopping.'

Grandma Bunn went to the Most Important Store in London, where the most Important people in London shopped. Through the smart glass doors she went past Perfumery, past Haberdashery, past Greengrocery – where Grand Ladies and the Duchesses in their glittering tiaras were pinching the lettuces, squeezing the melons, prodding the avocados, and poking their long aristocratic noses into the guanabanas – to Dress Materials.

'Please,' she told a Manager in a Pin Stripe Suit, 'I would like a yard of black bombazine, to make into a Best Dress for Sundays.'

The Manager in the Pin Stripe Suit looked offended. 'We *never* serve *rabbits*,' he said haughtily. Rabbits! Suddenly he was reminded of his favourite soup: dark, fragrant, bubbling-in-the-pot, *delicious* rabbit soup.

Grandma Bunn, who was sensitive to such thoughts,

quivered with rage. 'I'll give him rabbit soup!' she vowed. She hurried past Greengrocery – where the Grand Ladies and the Duchesses in their glittering tiaras were pinching the lettuces, squeezing the melons, prodding the avocados, and poking their long aristocratic noses into the guanabanas – past Haberdashery, past Perfumery, and out through the smart glass doors of the Most Important Store in London.

That night she returned, with Mummy Bunn, Violet and Hyacinth the Twins, and Daddy Bunn. They squeezed through the letter box, hurried past Perfumery, past Haberdashery, to Greengrocery, where they nibbled the lettuces, munched the melons, gnawed the avocados, and ate *ALL* of the guanabanas.

Next morning when they saw the nibbled lettuces, the munched melons, the gnawed avocados, and *NO* guanabanas, the Grand Ladies and the Duchesses swept past Haberdashery, past Perfumery, out of the smart glass doors and down the street, to the Second Most Important Store in London.

The Manager in the Pin Stripe Suit wrung his hands in despair. He tore out his hair by the handful.

'Poor Manager in the Pin Stripe Suit!' giggled Violet and Hyacinth the Twins.

'Fiddlesticks!' snapped Grandma Bunn. 'He had to be taught a lesson. He was thinking of *you-know-what*.'

'That was asking for trouble,' said Mummy Bunn.

'It's we who are asking for trouble,' said Daddy Bunn. 'We should have stayed at home.'

'Tush, Reginald!' snapped Grandma Bunn. 'Please,' she told the Manager in the Pin Stripe Suit, 'I would like a yard of black bombazine, to make into a Best Dress for Sundays.'

123

'Certainly Madam,' he replied, for he had learned his lesson. He would never again be rude to a rabbit. And not once did he think of rabbit soup, as he wrapped a yard of black bombazine in a neat package and gave it to Grandma Bunn.

Then past Greengrocery, past Haberdashery, past Perfumery, out of the smart glass doors, and along the streets of London went the Bobtail Bunns: Grandma Bunn, wearing her best straw hat with buttercups on it, and carrying an umbrella that was almost as tall as she was, and a yard of black bombazine done up in a neat package; plump Mummy Bunn; Violet and Hyacinth the Twins; and Daddy Bunn, wearing his best brown waistcoat and his usual worried expression. They returned to the garden of Buckingham Palace, where the First and Second Gardeners, and the Forbidding Third Gardener were waiting for them!

Straight away Mummy Bunn went in search of something to eat. She discovered a giant sunflower. Being partial to sunflower seeds, she scrambled up the thick stalk, and ate . . . and ate . . . and ate . . . until she was too topfull to eat any more. Then with a contented yawn, she stretched out on top of the giant sunflower and fell asleep.

The three gardeners crept towards the giant sunflower. The Forbidding Third Gardener reached up, and with a 'Got you, my plump beauty!' grabbed poor Mummy Bunn and popped her into a sack. Then the three gardeners hurried with Mummy Bunn to the kitchen, to have her made into rabbit stew.

Violet and Hyacinth the Twins ran to where Daddy Bunn had nodded off under the geraniums.

'You'll have to stir yourself, Our Dad!' they cried. 'The gardeners have taken Our Mum to the kitchen, to have her made into stew!'

'The disgrace of it!' wailed Daddy Bunn. 'A Bobtail Bunn finishing up in a stew! I knew we should have stayed at home.'

'Tush, Reginald!' scolded Grandma Bunn. 'What can you be thinking of! If Vanilla has been taken, you must rescue her.'

Poor wretched Reginald! 'I don't know anything about rescuing anyone,' he said.

'You had better take my umbrella,' said Grandma Bunn.

Daddy Bunn took the umbrella. Climbing on to the window sill, he peered into the kitchen. He saw the sack with Mummy Bunn inside it, and he saw the three gardeners. They were arguing with a Fat Cook.

'I like onions in my stew,' said the First Gardener.

'I don't like onions,' said the Forbidding Third Gardener.

'No onions, no stew!' said the Fat Cook firmly.

'Very well,' said the Forbidding Third Gardener. 'One onion.'

'I like celery in my stew,' said the Second Gardener.

'I don't like celery,' said the Forbidding Third Gardener.

'No celery, no stew!' said the Fat Cook firmly.

'Very well,' said the Forbidding Third Gardener. 'One stick of celery.'

Daddy Bunn hooked the curved handle of Grandma Bunn's umbrella round the neck of the sack with Mummy Bunn in it, and hauled the sack up and out of the kitchen window.

When the three gardeners realised that the sack was gone, they gave cries of rage.

'No rabbit, no stew!' said the Fat Cook firmly.

'You were quite right, Reginald,' said Grandma Bunn. 'We should have stayed at home.'

The Bobtail Bunns hurried from the garden of Buckingham Palace, and into the streets of London.

The people of London stared and nudged and whispered. But the Bobtail Bunns took no notice. Looking neither to right nor left they went on their way until they reached a Railway Station. There they boarded a train for Hutch End: Grandma Bunn, wearing her best straw hat with buttercups on it, and carrying an umbrella that was almost as tall as she was, and a yard of black bombazine done up in a neat parcel; plump Mummy Bunn, carrying a munch-bag filled with carrots for the journey; Violet and Hyacinth the Twins; and Daddy Bunn, wearing his best brown waistcoat and a pleased to be-going-home-again expression.

Elizabeth Robinson

The Jumblies

They went to sea in a Sieve, they did,
   In a Sieve they went to sea:
In spite of all their friends could say,
On a winter's morn, on a stormy day,
   In a Sieve they went to sea!
And when the Sieve turned round and round
And every one cried, 'You'll all be drowned!'
They called aloud, 'Our Sieve ain't big,
But we don't care a button! we don't care a fig!
   In a Sieve we'll go to sea!'
     Far and few, far and few,
       Are the lands where the Jumblies live;
       Their heads are green, and their hands are blue,
       And they went to sea in a Sieve.

They sailed away in a Sieve, they did,
   In a Sieve they sailed so fast,
With only a beautiful pea-green veil
Tied with a riband by way of a sail,
   To a small tobacco-pipe mast;
And every one said, who saw them go,
'O won't they be soon upset, you know!
For the sky is dark, and the voyage is long,
And happen what may, it's extremely wrong
   In a Sieve to sail so fast!'
     Far and few, far and few,
       Are the lands where the Jumblies live;
       Their heads are green, and their hands are blue,
       And they went to sea in a Sieve.

The water it soon came in, it did,
    The water it soon came in;
So to keep them dry, they wrapped their feet
In a pinky paper all folded neat,
    And they fastened it down with a pin.
And they passed the night in a crockery-jar,
And each of them said, 'How wise we are!
Though the sky be dark, and the voyage be long,
Yet we never can think we were rash or wrong,
    While round in our Sieve we spin!'
        Far and few, far and few,
            Are the lands where the Jumblies live;
        Their heads are green, and their hands are blue,
            And they went to sea in a Sieve.

And all night long they sailed away;
    And when the sun went down,
They whistled and warbled a moony song
To the echoing sound of a coppery gong,
    In the shade of the mountains brown.
'O Timballo! How happy we are,
When we live in a Sieve and a crockery-jar,
And all night long in the moonlight pale,
We sail away with a pea-green sail,
    In the shade of the mountains brown!'
        Far and few, far and few,
            Are the lands where the Jumblies live;
        Their heads are green, and their hands are blue,
            And they went to sea in a Sieve.

They sailed to the Western Sea, they did,
  To a land all covered with trees,
And they bought an Owl, and a useful Cart,
And a pound of Rice, and a Cranberry Tart,
  And a hive of silvery Bees.
And they bought a Pig, and some green Jack-daws,
And a lovely Monkey with lollipop paws,
And forty bottles of Ring-Bo-Ree,
  And no end of Stilton Cheese.
    Far and few, far and few,
      Are the lands where the Jumblies live;
    Their heads are green, and their hands are blue,
      And they went to sea in a Sieve.

And in twenty years they all came back,
  In twenty years or more,
And every one said, 'How tall they've grown!
For they've been to the Lakes, and the Terrible
    Zone,
  And the hills of the Chankly Bore';
And they drank their health, and gave them a feast
Of dumplings made of beautiful yeast;
And every one said, 'If we only live,
We too will go to sea in a Sieve, –
  To the hills of the Chankly Bore!'
    Far and few, far and few,
      Are the lands where the Jumblies live;
    Their heads are green, and their hands are blue,
      And they went to sea in a Sieve.

Edward Lear

The Emperor's New Clothes

Many years ago there lived an Emperor who cared more
for beautiful clothes than for anything else in the world.
He took no interest in his army or his navy; it did not
amuse him to go out hunting, or to attend performances
in the theatre. What he liked best was to buy hundreds
and hundreds of new and gorgeous garments, and then
to strut forth among the people so that they might all
admire him. He had a different coat for every hour of the
day; and, just as in other countries a King is said to be in
his council-chamber, this Emperor was said to be 'in the
wardrobe'.

One day two bold and clever rascals arrived in the
capital city of the Empire. They said that they were
weavers, the most skilful ever known. Not only could
they weave fabrics of lovely colours and designs; their
handiwork possessed a magical quality. Nobody who
was very stupid could see it at all! And if clothes made

from this stuff were worn by anyone who was unfit for the office he held, they at once became invisible to everyone, including himself.

The Emperor was greatly interested, and the fame of the weavers spread all through the city. It was decided that a suit of clothes should be made for his Imperial Majesty as fast as the cloth could be woven.

'Now,' thought the Emperor, 'I shall soon find out which of my officers and ministers are unfit for their posts. Only intelligent men will be able to see my new clothes.'

So he gave the two mock-weavers large sums of money, and bade them start work at once. They set up two large looms, and drew the shuttles to and fro as if they were weaving; but there was nothing on the looms or in the shuttles.

They at once demanded the finest silk and the costliest gold; this they put into their own pockets, and worked at the empty looms till late into the night.

'I should like to know how far they have got on with the cloth,' thought the Emperor. But he felt somewhat uneasy when he thought that those who were not fit for their offices could not see it. He believed, indeed, that he had nothing to fear for himself, but yet he preferred first to send someone else to see how matters stood.

'I will send my honest old Minister to the weavers,' thought the Emperor. 'He can judge best how the stuff looks, for he has sense, and no one understands how to deal with others better than he.'

And so the good old Minister went into the hall where the two cheats sat working at the empty looms.

'Mercy preserve us!' thought the old Minister, and he

opened his eyes wide. 'I cannot see anything at all!' But he did not say this.

Both the cheats begged him to be kind enough to come nearer, and ask if he did not approve of the colours and the pattern. They pointed to the empty loom, and the poor old Minister went on opening his eyes; but he could see nothing, for there was nothing to see.

'Mercy!' thought he, 'can I indeed be so stupid? I never thought; not a soul must know it. Am I not fit for my office? – No, it will never do for me to say that I could not see the cloth.'

'What do you say?' said one of the weavers.

'Oh, it is charming – quite charming!' answered the old Minister, as he peered through his spectacles. 'What a fine pattern, and what colours! Yes, I shall tell the Emperor that I am very much pleased with it.'

'Well, we are glad of that,' said both the weavers; and then they named the colours, and explained the strange pattern. The old Minister listened attentively, that he might be able to repeat it when the Emperor came. And he did so.

Now the cheats asked for more money, and more silk and gold, which they declared they wanted for weaving. They put all into their own pockets, and not a thread was put upon the loom; but they pretended to work at the empty frames as before.

The Emperor soon sent another honest councillor to see how the weaving was going on, and if the suit would soon be ready. He fared just like the first: he looked and looked, but, as there was nothing to be seen but the empty looms, for all his looking – he could see nothing.

'Is not that a pretty piece of cloth?' asked the two rascals, and they displayed and explained the handsome pattern which was not there at all.

'I am not stupid!' thought the man; 'It must be my good office, for which I am not fit. It is odd indeed, but I must not let it be noticed.' And so he praised the cloth which he did not see, and expressed his pleasure at the beautiful colours and the charming pattern. 'Yes, it is enchanting,' he said to the Emperor.

All the people in the town were talking of the tailors and their wonderful cloth. The Emperor wished to see the material himself while it was still upon the loom. With a whole crowd of chosen men, he went to the two cunning cheats, who were now weaving with might and main without fibre or thread.

'Is that not splendid?' said the two old councillors who had already been there once. 'Does not your Majesty note the pattern and the colours?'

And then they pointed to the empty loom, for they thought that others could see the cloth.

'What's this?' thought the Emperor. 'I can see nothing at all! That is terrible. Am I stupid? Am I not fit to be Emperor? That would be the most dreadful thing that could happen to me. – Oh, it is *very* pretty!' he said aloud. 'It has our complete approval.' And he nodded in a contented way, and gazed at the empty loom, for he would not say that he saw nothing. His whole suite looked and looked, and saw nothing, any more than the rest; but, like the Emperor, they said, 'That is pretty!' and counselled him to wear these splendid new clothes for the first time at the great procession that was presently to take place. 'It is splendid, tasteful, excellent!' went from mouth to mouth. On all sides there seemed to be general rejoicing, and the Emperor gave the rascals the title of Imperial Court Weavers.

The whole night before the morning on which the procession was to take place the cheats were up, and had lighted more than sixteen candles. The people could see that they were hard at work, completing the Emperor's new clothes. They pretended to take the stuff down from the loom; they made cuts in the air with great scissors; they sewed with needles without thread; and at last they said, 'Now the clothes are ready!'

The Emperor came himself with the lords of his Court; and the two cheats lifted up one arm as if they were holding something, and said, 'See, here are the trousers! Here is the coat! Here is the cloak!' and so on. 'It is as light as a spider's web: one would think one had nothing on; but that is just the beauty of it.'

'Yes,' said all the noble lords; but they could not see anything, for nothing was there.

'Does your Imperial Majesty please condescend to undress?' said the cheats; 'then we will put on you the new clothes here in front of the great mirror.'

The Emperor took off his outer clothes, and the cheats pretended to put on him each new garment as it was ready; and the Emperor turned round and round before the mirror.

'Oh, how well they look! How splendidly they fit!' said all. 'What a pattern! What colours! That *is* a splendid robe!'

'The attendants are waiting outside with the canopy which is to be borne above your Majesty in the procession!' announced the master of the ceremonies.

'Well, I am ready,' replied the Emperor. 'Does it not suit me well?' And then he turned again to the mirror,

for he wanted it to appear as if he were looking at his attire with great interest.

The chamberlains who were to carry the train stooped down with their hands towards the floor, just as if they were picking up the robe; then they pretended to be holding something in the air. They did not dare to let it be noticed that they saw nothing.

So the Emperor went in procession under the rich canopy, and every one in the streets said, 'How incomparable are the Emperor's new clothes! What a rich train he has to his robe! How well it fits him!' No one would let it be known that he could see nothing, for that would have proved that he was either very stupid or quite unfit for the office he held. No clothes of the Emperor's had ever been so much admired as these which nobody could see!

At last, however, a small child in the crowd cried out, 'But he has nothing on!'

'Listen to this foolish child!' said the father, laughing. But the child's words ran from one onlooker to another, till all the people were murmuring, 'He has nothing on!'

These murmurs reached the ears of the Emperor, and alarmed him not a little, for he thought there must be some truth in them. Still, he could not stop in the middle of the procession. So he marched on, even more proudly than before, and the chamberlains lifted higher than ever the train which did not exist at all.

Hans Andersen

The Knight's Song

I'll tell thee everything I can:
    There's little to relate.
I saw an aged aged man,
    A-sitting on a gate.
'Who are you, aged man?' I said.
    'And how is it you live?'
And his answer trickled through my head
    Like water through a sieve.

He said, 'I look for butterflies
    That sleep among the wheat:
I make them into mutton-pies,
    And sell them in the street.
I sell them unto men,' he said,
    'Who sail on stormy seas;
And that's the way I get my bread –
    A trifle, if you please.'

But I was thinking of a plan
    To dye one's whiskers green,
And always use so large a fan
    That they could not be seen.
So, having no reply to give
    To what the old man said
I cried 'Come, tell me how you live!'
    And thumped him on the head.

His accents mild took up the tale:
    He said 'I go my ways,
And when I find a mountain-rill,

I set in in a blaze;
And thence they make a stuff they call
  Rowland's Macassar Oil –
Yet twopence-halfpenny is all
  They give me for my toil.'

But I was thinking of a way
  To feed oneself on batter,
And so go on from day to day
  Getting a little fatter.
I shook him well from side to side,
  Until his face was blue:
'Come, tell me how you live,' I cried,
  'And what it is you do!'

He said, 'I hunt for haddock's eyes
  Among the heather bright,
And work them into waistcoat-buttons
  In the silent night.
And these I do not sell for gold
  Or coin of silvery shine
But for a copper halfpenny,
  And that will purchase nine.

'I sometimes dig for buttered rolls,
  Or set limed twigs for crabs:
I sometimes search the grassy knolls
  For wheels of hansom-cabs.
And that's the way (he gave a wink)
  By which I get my wealth –
And very gladly will I drink
  Your Honour's noble health.'

I heard him then, for I had just
   Completed my design
To keep the Menai bridge from rust
   By boiling it in wine.
I thanked him much for telling me
   The way he got his wealth,
But chiefly for his wish that he
   Might drink my noble health.

And now, if e'er by chance I put
   My fingers into glue,
Or madly squeeze a right-hand foot
   Into a left-hand shoe,
Or if I drop upon my toe
   A very heavy weight,
I weep, for it reminds me so
Of that old man I used to know –
Whose look was mild, whose speech was slow,
Whose hair was whiter than the snow,
Whose face was very like a crow,
With eyes, like cinders, all aglow,
Who seemed distracted with his woe,
Who rocked his body to and fro,
And muttered mumblingly and low,
As if his mouth were full of dough,
Who snorted like a buffalo –
That summer evening long ago,
   A-sitting on a gate.

Lewis Carroll

There Was an Old Woman
Who Lived in a Shoe

There was an old woman who lived in a shoe,
She had so many children she didn't know what to do;
She gave them some broth, without any bread,
She whipped them all soundly, and sent them to bed.

Two Little Kittens

Two little kittens
One stormy night,
Began to quarrel,
And then to fight.

One had a mouse
And the other had none;
And that was the way
The quarrel begun.

'I'll have that mouse,'
Said the bigger cat.
'You'll have that mouse?
We'll see about that!'

'I will have that mouse,'
Said the tortoise-shell;
And, sitting and scratching,
On her sister she fell.

I've told you before
'Twas a stormy night,
When these two kittens
Began to fight.

The old woman took
The sweeping broom,
And swept them both
Right out of the room.

The ground was covered
With frost and snow,
They had lost the mouse,
And had nowhere to go.

So they lay and shivered
Beside the door,
Till the old woman finished
Sweeping the floor.

And then they crept in
As quiet as mice,
All wet with snow
And as cold as ice.

They found it much better
That stormy night,
To lie by the fire,
Than to quarrel and fight.

Jane Taylor

THE VALIANT TIN SOLDIER

There were once five and twenty tin soldiers; they were all brothers, for they had all been born of one old tin spoon. They shouldered their muskets, and looked straight before them: their uniform was red and blue, and very splendid. The first thing they had heard in the world, when the lid was taken off their box, had been the words 'Tin soldiers!' These words were uttered by a little boy, clapping his hands; the soldiers had been given to him, for it was his birthday; and now he put them upon the table. Each soldier was exactly like the rest; but one of them had been cast last of all, and there had not been enough tin to finish him; but he stood as firmly upon his one leg as the others on their two; and it was just this soldier who became remarkable.

On the table on which they had been placed stood many other playthings, but the toy that attracted most attention was a neat castle of cardboard. Through the little windows one could see straight into the hall. Before

the castle some little trees were placed round a little looking-glass, which was to represent a clear lake. Waxen swans swam on this lake, and were mirrored in it. This was all very pretty; but the prettiest of all was a little lady, who stood at the open door of the castle: she was also cut out in paper, but she had a dress of the clearest gauze, and a little narrow blue ribbon over her shoulders that looked like a scarf; and in the middle of this ribbon was a shining tinsel rose as big as her whole face. The little lady stretched out both her arms, for she was a dancer; and then she lifted one leg so high that the tin soldier could not see it at all, and thought that, like himself, she had but one leg.

'That would be the wife for me,' thought he; 'but she is very grand. She lives in a castle, and I have only a box, and there are five and twenty of us in that. It is no place for her. But I must try to make acquaintance with her.'

And then he lay down at full length behind a snuff-box which was on the table; there he could easily watch the dainty little lady, who continued to stand on one leg without losing her balance.

When the evening came, all the other tin soldiers were put into their box, and the people in the house went to bed. Now the toys began to play. The tin soldiers rattled in their box for they wanted to join, but could not lift the lid. The nutcracker threw somersaults, and the pencil amused itself on the table: there was so much noise that the canary woke up, and began to speak too, and even in verse.

The only two who did not stir from their places were the tin soldier and the dancing lady: she stood straight up on the point of one of her toes, and stretched out both her arms; and he was just as strong on his one leg; and he never turned his eyes away from her.

Now the clock struck twelve – and, *bounce !* – the lid flew off the snuff-box; but there was not snuff in it, but a little goblin: you see it was a trick.

'Tin soldier!' said the goblin, 'don't stare at things that don't concern you.'

But the tin soldier pretended not to hear him.

'Just you wait till tomorrow!' said the goblin.

But when the morning came, and the children got up, the tin soldier was placed in the window; and whether it was the goblin or the draught that did it, all at once the window flew open, and the soldier fell head over heels out of the third storey. That was a terrible tumble! He put his legs straight up, and stuck his helmet downward and his bayonet between the paving stones.

The servant-maid and the little boy came down directly to look for him, but though they almost trod upon him they could not see him. If the soldier had cried out, 'Here I am!' they would have found him; but he did not think it fitting to call out loudly, because he was in uniform.

Now it began to rain; the drops soon fell thicker, and at last it came down in a complete stream. When the rain was over two boys came by.

'Just look!' said one of them, 'there lies a tin soldier. He must come out and ride in the boat.'

And they made a boat out of a newspaper, and put the tin soldier in the middle of it; and so he sailed down the gutter, and the two boys ran beside him and clapped their hands. Goodness preserve us! how the waves rose in that gutter, and how fast the stream ran! But then it had been a heavy rain. The paper boat rocked up and down, and sometimes turned round so rapidly that the tin soldier trembled; but he remained firm, and never changed countenance, and looked straight before him, and shouldered his musket.

All at once the boat went into a long drain, and it became as dark as if he had been in his box.

'Where am I going now?' he thought. 'Yes, yes, that's the goblin's fault. Ah! if the little lady only sat here with me in the boat, it might be twice as dark for all that I should care.'

Suddenly there came a great water rat, which lived in the drain.

'Have you a passport?' said the rat. 'Give me your passport.'

But the tin soldier kept silence, and held his musket tighter than ever.

The boat went on, but the rat came after it. *Hu!* how he gnashed his teeth, and called out to the bits of straw and wood:

'Hold him! hold him! he hasn't paid toll – he hasn't shown his passport!'

But the stream became stronger and stronger.

The tin soldier could see the bright daylight where the arch ended; but he heard a roaring noise, which might well have frightened a bolder man.

Only think – just where the tunnel ended, the drain ran into a great canal; and for him that would have been as dangerous as for us to be carried down a great water-fall.

Now he was already so near it that he could not stop.

The boat was carried out, the poor tin soldier stiffening himself as much as he could, and no one could say that he moved an eyelid.

The boat whirled round three or four times, and was full of water to the very edge – it must sink. The tin soldier stood up to his neck in water, and the boat sank deeper and deeper, and the paper was loosened more and more; and now the water closed over the soldier's head. Then he thought of the pretty little dancer, and how he would never see her again; and it sounded in the soldier's ears:

> Farewell, farewell, thou warrior brave,
> For this day thou must die!

And now the paper parted, and the tin soldier fell out; but at that moment he was snapped up by a great fish.

Oh, how dark it was in that fish's body! It was darker than in the drain tunnel; and then it was very narrow too. But the tin soldier remained unmoved, and lay at full length shouldering his musket.

The fish swam to and fro, he made the most wonderful movements, and then became quite still. At last something flashed through him like lightning. The daylight shone quite clear, and a voice said aloud, 'The Tin Soldier!' The fish had been caught, carried to market, bought, and taken into the kitchen, where the cook cut him open with a large knife. She seized the soldier round his body with both her hands, and carried him into the room, where all were anxious to see the remarkable man who had travelled about in the inside of a fish; but the tin soldier was not at all proud. They placed him on the table, and there – ! What curious things may happen in this world! The tin soldier was in the very room in which he had been before! He saw the same children, and the same toys stood on the table; and there was the pretty castle with the graceful little dancer. She was still balancing herself on one leg, and held the other extended in the air. She was hardy too. That moved the tin soldier; he was very nearly weeping tin tears, but that would not have been proper. He looked at her, but they said nothing to each other.

Then one of the little boys took the tin soldier and flung him into the stove. He gave no reason for doing this. It must have been the fault of the goblin in the snuff-box.

The tin soldier stood there quite illuminated, and felt a heat that was terrible; but whether this heat proceeded from the real fire or from love he did not know. The colours had quite gone off from him; but whether that had happened on the journey, or had been caused by grief, no one could say. He looked at the little lady, she looked at him, and he felt that he was melting; but he still stood firm, shouldering his musket. Then suddenly

the door flew open, and the draught of air caught the dancer, and she flew like a sylph just into the stove to the tin soldier, and flashed up in a flame, and she was gone. Then the tin soldier melted down into a lump, and when the servant-maid took the ashes out next day she found him in the shape of a little tin heart. But of the dancer nothing remained but the tinsel rose, and that was burned as black as coal.

Hans Andersen

THE UGLY DUCKLING

It was glorious out in the country. It was summer. All around the fields and meadows were great forests, and in the midst of these forests lay deep lakes. Yes, it was really glorious out in the country. In the midst of the sunshine there lay an old farm, surrounded by deep canals, and from the wall down to the water grew great burdocks, so high that little children could stand upright under the loftiest of them. It was just as wild there as in the deepest wood. Here sat a duck upon her nest, for she had to hatch her young ones; but she was almost tired out before the little ones came; and then she so seldom had visitors. The other ducks liked better to swim in the canals than to run up to sit down under a burdock, and cackle with her.

At last one egg-shell after another burst open. '*Peep ! peep !*' it cried, and in all the eggs there were little creatures that stuck out their heads.

'*Rap ! rap !*' they said; and they all came rapping out

as fast as they could, looking all round them under the green leaves; and the mother let them look as much as they chose, for green is good for the eyes.

'How wide the world is!' said the young ones, for they certainly had much more room now than when they were in the eggs.

'Do you think this is all the world?' asked the mother. 'That extends far across the other side of the garden, quite into the parson's field, but I have never been there yet. I hope you are all together,' she continued, and stood up. 'No, I have not all. The largest egg still lies there. How long is that to last? I am really tired of it.' And she sat down again.

'Well, how are you?' asked an old duck who had come to pay her a visit.

'It lasts a long time with that one egg,' said the duck who sat there. 'It will not burst. Now, only look at the others; are they not the prettiest ducks one could possibly see? They are all like their father: the bad fellow, by the way, never comes to see me.'

'Let me see the egg which will not burst,' said the old visitor. 'Believe me, it is a turkey's egg. I was once cheated in that way, and had much anxiety and trouble with the young ones, for they are afraid of the water. I could not get them to venture in. I quacked and clucked, but it was no use. Let me see the egg. Yes, that's a turkey's egg! Let it lie there, and teach the other children to swim.'

'I think I will sit on it a little longer,' said the duck. 'I've sat so long now that I can sit a few days more.'

'Just as you please,' said the old duck; and she went away.

At last the great egg burst. '*Peep ! peep !*' said the little one, and crept forth. It was very large and very ugly. The duck looked at it.

'It's a very large duckling,' said she; 'none of the others look like that : can it really be a turkey chick ? Now we shall soon find out. It must go into the water, even if I have to thrust it in myself.'

The next day the weather was splendidly bright, and the sun shone on all the green trees. The mother-duck went down to the water with all her little ones. *Splash* she jumped into the water. '*Quack ! quack !*' she said, and one duckling after another plunged in. The water closed over their heads, but they came up in an instant, and swam capitally; their legs went by themselves, and there they were all in the water. The ugly grey duckling swam with them.

'No, it's not a turkey,' said she; 'look how well it can use its legs, and how upright it holds itself. It is my own child! On the whole it's quite pretty, if one looks at it rightly. *Quack ! quack !* come with me, and I'll lead you out into the great world, and present you in the poultry-yard; but keep close to me, so that no one may tread on you; and take care of the cats!'

And so they came into the poultry-yard. There was a terrible riot going on in there, for two families were quarrelling about an eel's head, and the cat got it after all.

'See, that's how it goes in the world!' said the mother-duck; and she whetted her beak, for she, too, wanted the eel's head. 'Only use your legs,' she said. 'See that you can bustle about, and bow your heads before the old duck yonder. She's the grandest of all here; she's of Spanish blood – that's why she's so fat; and do you see,

she has a red rag round her leg; that's something par-
ticularly fine. Shake yourselves – don't turn in your toes;
a well-brought-up duck turns its toes quite out, just like
father and mother, so! Now bend your necks and say
"*Rap!*"'

And they did so; but the other ducks round about
looked at them, and said quite boldly:

'Look there! Now we're to have these hanging on as if
there were not enough of us already! And – fie! – how
that duckling yonder looks; we won't stand that!'
And one duck flew up immediately, and bit it in the
neck.

'Let it alone,' said the mother; 'it does no harm to
anyone.'

'Yes, but it's too large and peculiar,' said the duck
who had bitten it; 'and therefore it must be buffeted.'

'Those are pretty children that the mother has there,'
said the old duck with the rag round her leg. 'They're all
pretty but that one; that was a failure. I wish she could
alter it.'

'That cannot be done, my lady,' replied the mother-
duck. 'It is not pretty, but it has a really good disposition,
and swims as well as any other; I may even say it swims
better. I think it will grow up pretty, and become smaller
in time; it has lain too long in the egg, and therefore is
not properly shaped.' And then she pinched it in the
neck, and smoothed its feathers. 'Moreover, it is a drake,'
she said, 'and therefore it is not of much consequence.
I think he will be very strong; he makes his way
already.'

'The other ducklings are graceful enough,' said the
old duck. 'Make yourself at home; and if you find an eel's
head, you may bring it me.'

And now they were at home. But the poor duckling which had crept last out of the egg, and looked so ugly, was bitten and pushed and jeered, as much by the ducks as by the chickens.

'It is too big!' they all said. And the turkey-cock, who had been born with spurs, and therefore thought himself an emperor, blew himself up like a ship in full sail, and bore straight down upon it; then he gobbled, and grew quite red in the face. The poor duckling did not know where it should stand or walk; it was quite miserable because it looked ugly and was scoffed at by the whole yard.

So it went on the first day; and afterward it became worse and worse. The poor duckling was pushed about by everyone; even its brothers and sisters were quite angry with it, and said: 'If the cat would only catch you, you ugly creature!' And the mother said, 'If you were only far away!' And the ducks bit it, and the chickens beat it, and the girl who had to feed the poultry kicked at it with her foot.

Then it ran and flew over the fence, and the little birds in the bushes flew up in fear.

'That is because I am so ugly!' thought the duckling; and it shut its eyes, but flew on farther; thus it came out into the great moor, where the wild ducks lived. Here it lay the whole night long; and it was weary and downcast.

Towards morning the wild ducks flew up, and looked at their new companion.

'What sort of a one are you?' they asked; and the duckling turned in every direction, and bowed as well as it could. 'You are remarkably ugly!' said the wild ducks. 'But that does not matter to us, so long as you do not marry into our family.'

Poor thing! It certainly did not think of marrying, and only hoped to obtain leave to lie among the reeds and drink some of the swamp water.

Thus it lay two whole days; then came thither two wild geese, or, properly speaking, two wild ganders. It was not long since each had crept out of an egg, and that's why they were so saucy.

'Listen, friend,' said one of them. 'You're so ugly that I like you. Near here, in another moor, there are a few sweet lovely wild geese, all unmarried, and all able to say "*Rap!*" You've a chance of making your fortune, ugly as you are!'

'*Piff! paff*' resounded through the air; and the two ganders fell down dead in the swamp, and the water became blood-red. '*Piff! Paff!*' it sounded again, and whole flocks of wild geese rose up from the reeds. And then there was another shot. A great hunt was going on. The hunters were lying in wait all round the moor, and some were even sitting up in the branches of the trees, which spread far over the reeds. The blue smoke rose up like clouds among the dark trees, and was wafted far away across the water; and the hunting dogs came – *splash, splash!* – into the swamp, and the rushes and the reeds bent down on every side. That was a fright for the poor duckling! It turned its head, and put it under its wing; but at that moment a frightful great dog stood close by the duckling. His tongue hung far out of his mouth and his eyes gleamed horrible and ugly; he thrust out his nose close against the duckling, showed his sharp teeth, and – *splash, splash!* – on he went, without seizing it.

'Oh, Heaven be thanked!' sighed the duckling. 'I am so ugly that even the dog does not like to bite me!'

And so it lay quite quiet, while the shots rattled through the reeds and gun after gun was fired. At last, late in the day, silence was restored; but the poor duckling did not dare to rise up; it waited several hours before it looked round, and then hastened away out of the moor as fast as it could. It ran on over field and meadow; there was such a storm raging that it was difficult to get from one place to another.

Towards evening the duckling came to a little miserable peasant's hut. This hut was so tumbledown that it did not know on which side it should fall; and that's why it remained standing. The storm whistled round the duckling in such a way that the poor creature was obliged to sit down, to stand against it; and the tempest grew worse and worse. Then the duckling noticed that one of the hinges of the door had given way, and the door hung so slanting that the duckling could slip through the crack into the room; and it did so.

Here lived a woman, with her tomcat and her hen. And the tomcat, whom she called Sonnie, could arch his back and purr, he could even give out sparks – but for that one had to stroke his fur the wrong way. The hen had quite little short legs and therefore she was called Chickabiddyshortshanks; she laid good eggs, and the women loved her as if she were her own child.

In the morning the strange duckling was at once noticed, and the tomcat began to purr, and the hen to cluck.

'What's this?' said the woman, and looked all round; but she could not see well, and therefore she thought the duckling was a fat duck that had strayed. 'This is a rare prize!' she said. 'Now I shall have duck's eggs. I hope it is not a drake. We must try that.'

And so the duckling was admitted on trial for three weeks; but no eggs came.

'Can you lay eggs?' asked the hen.

'No.'

'Then you'll have the goodness to hold your tongue.'

And the tomcat said, 'Can you curve your back, and purr, and give out sparks?'

'No.'

'Then you cannot have any opinion of your own when sensible people are speaking.'

And the duckling sat in a corner and was miserable; then the fresh air and the sunshine streamed in; and it was seized with such a strange longing to swim on the water that it could not help telling the hen of it.

'What are you thinking of?' cried the hen. 'You have nothing to do, that's why you have these fancies. Purr or lay eggs, and they will pass over.'

'But it is so charming to swim on the water!' said the duckling, 'so refreshing to let it close above one's head, and to dive down to the bottom.'

'Yes, that must be a mighty pleasure truly,' said the hen. 'I fancy you must have gone crazy. Ask the cat about it – he's the cleverest animal I know – ask him if he likes to swim on the water, or to dive down: I won't speak about myself. Ask our mistress, the old woman; no one in the world is cleverer than she. Do you think she has any desire to swim, and to let the water close above her head?'

'You don't understand me,' said the duckling.

'We don't understand you? Then pray who is to understand you? You surely don't pretend to be cleverer than the tomcat and the woman – I won't say anything of myself. Don't be conceited, child, and be grateful for all the kindness you have received. Did you not get into a warm room, and have you not fallen into company from which you may learn something? But you are a chatterer, and it is not pleasant to associate with you. You may believe me, I speak for your good. I tell you disagreeable things, and by that one may always know one's true friends! Only take care that you learn to lay eggs, or to purr and give out sparks!'

'I think I will go out into the wide world,' said the duckling.

'Yes, do go,' replied the hen.

And the duckling went away. It swam on the water, and dived, but it was slighted by every creature because of its ugliness.

Now came the autumn. The leaves in the forest turned yellow and brown; the wind caught them so that they danced about, and up in the air it was very cold. The clouds hung low, heavy with hail and snowflakes, and on the fence stood the raven, crying, '*Croak ! croak !*' from mere cold; yes, it was enough to make one feel cold to think of this. The poor little duckling certainly had a bad time. One evening – the sun was just setting in his beauty – there came a whole flock of great handsome birds out of the bushes; they were dazzling white, with long flexible necks; they were swans. They uttered a very peculiar cry, spread forth their glorious great wings, and flew away from that cold region to warmer lands, to fair open lakes. They mounted so high, so high! and the ugly little duckling felt quite strangely as it watched them. It turned round and round in the water like a wheel, stretched out its neck towards them, and uttered such a strange loud cry as frightened itself. Oh! it could not forget those beautiful, happy birds; and so soon as it could see them no longer, it dived down to the very bottom, and when it came up again, it was quite beside itself. It knew not the name of those birds, and knew not whither they were flying; but it loved them more than it had ever loved anyone. It was not at all envious of them. How could it think of wishing to possess such loveliness as they had? It would have been glad if only the ducks would have endured its company – the poor ugly creature!

And the winter grew cold, very cold! The duckling was forced to swim about in the water, to prevent the surface from freezing entirely; but every night the hole in which it swam about became smaller and smaller. It froze so hard that the icy covering crackled again; and the duckling was obliged to use its legs continually to prevent the hole from freezing up. At last it became exhausted, and lay quite still, and thus froze fast into the ice.

Early in the morning a peasant came by, and when he saw what had happened, he took his wooden shoe, broke the ice-crust to pieces, and carried the duckling home to his wife. Then it came to itself again. The children wanted to play with it; but the duckling thought they would do it an injury, and in its terror fluttered up into the milk-pan, so that the milk spurted down into the room. The woman clapped her hands, at which the duckling flew down into the butter-tub, and then into the meal-barrel and out again. How it looked then! The woman screamed and struck at it with the fire-tongs; the children tumbled over one another in their efforts to catch the duckling; and they laughed and screamed finely! Happily the door stood open, and the poor creature was able to slip out between the shrubs into the newly fallen snow; and there it lay quite exhausted.

But it would be too sad if I were to tell all the misery and care which the duckling had to endure in the hard winter. It lay out on the moor among the reeds, when the sun began to shine again and the larks to sing: it was a beautiful spring.

Then all at once the duckling could flap its wings: they beat the air more strongly than before, and bore it strongly away; and before it knew how all this happened, it found itself in a great garden, where the elder-trees smelt sweet, and bent their long green branches down to the canal that wound through the region. Oh, here it was so beautiful, such a gladness of spring! and from the thicket came three glorious white swans; they rustled their wings, and swam lightly on the water. The duckling knew the splendid creatures, and felt oppressed by a peculiar sadness.

'I will fly away to them, to the royal birds! and they will kill me, because I, that am so ugly, dare to approach them. But it is of no consequence! Better to be killed by them than to be pursued by ducks, and beaten by fowls, and pushed about by the girl who takes care of the poultry-yard, and to suffer hunger in winter!' And it flew out into the water, and swam towards the beautiful swans: these looked at it, and came sailing down upon it with outspread wings. 'Kill me!' said the poor creature, and bent its head down upon the water, expecting nothing but death. But what was this that it saw in the clear water? It beheld its own image; and, lo! it was no longer a clumsy dark grey bird, ugly and hateful to look at, but – a swan!

It felt quite glad at all the need and misfortune it had suffered, now it realised its happiness in all the splendour that surrounded it. And the great swans swam round it, and stroked it with their beaks.

Into the garden came little children, who threw bread

and corn into the water; and the youngest cried, 'There is a new one!' and the other children shouted joyously, 'Yes, a new one has arrived!' And they clapped their hands and danced about, and ran to their father and mother; and bread and cake were thrown into the water; and they all said, 'The new one is the most beautiful of all! so young and handsome!' and the old swans bowed their heads before him.

Then he felt quite ashamed, and hid his head under his wings, for he did not know what to do; he was so happy, and yet not at all proud. He thought how he had been persecuted and despised; and now he heard them saying that he was the most beautiful of all birds. Even the elder-tree bent its branches straight down into the water before him, and the sun shone warm and mild. Then his wings rustled, he lifted his slender neck, and cried rejoicingly from the depths of his heart:

'I never dreamed of so much happiness when I was just an ugly duckling!'

The Hump

The Camel's hump is an ugly lump
 Which well you may see at the Zoo;
But uglier yet is the hump we get
 From having too little to do.

Kiddies and grown-ups too-oo-oo,
If we haven't enough to do-oo-oo,
  We get the hump –
  Cameelious hump –
The hump that is black and blue!

We climb out of bed with a frouzly head
 And a snarly-yarly voice.
We shiver and scowl and we grunt and we growl
 At our bath and our boots and our toys;

And there ought to be a corner for me
(And I know there is one for you)
  When we get the hump –
  Cameelious hump –
The hump that is black and blue!

The cure for this ill is not to sit still,
 Or frowst with a book by the fire;
But to take a large hoe and a shovel also,
 And dig till you gently perspire;

And then you will find that the sun and the wind,
And the Djinn of the garden too,

Have lifted the hump –
The horrible hump –
The hump that is black and blue!

I get it as well as you-oo-oo-
If I haven't enough to do-oo-oo!
We all get hump –
Cameelious hump –
Kiddies and grown-ups too!

Rudyard Kipling

The Spider

How doth the jolly little spider
Wind up such miles of silk inside her?
The explanation seems to be
She does not eat so much as me.

And if I never, never cram
Myself with ginger-bread and jam,
Then maybe I'll have room to hide
A little rope in *my* inside.

Then I shall tie it very tight
Just over the electric light,
And hang head downward from the ceiling –
I wonder if one *minds* the feeling?

Or else I'd tie it to a tree
And let myself into the sea;
But when I wound it up again
I wonder if I'd have a pain?

A. P. Herbert

Tom Thumb

There was once a poor woodman sitting by the fire in his cottage, and his wife sat by his side spinning.

'How lonely it is,' said he, 'for you and me to sit here by ourselves without any children to play about us and to amuse us, while other people seem so happy and merry with their children!'

'What you say is very true,' said the wife, sighing and turning round her wheel; 'how happy should I be if I had but one child! and if it were ever so small, nay, if it were no bigger than my thumb, I should be very happy, and love it dearly.'

Now it came to pass that this good woman's wish was fulfilled just as she desired, for some time afterward she had a little boy who was quite healthy and strong, but not much bigger than my thumb.

So they said, 'Well, we cannot say we have not got what we wished for, and, little as he is, we will love him dearly'; and they called him Tom Thumb.

168

They gave him plenty of food, yet he never grew bigger, but remained just the same size as when he was born; still his eyes were sharp and sparkling, and he soon showed himself to be a clever little fellow, who always knew well what he was about. One day, as the woodman was getting ready to go into the wood to cut fuel, he said,

'I wish I had some one to bring the cart after me, for I want to make haste.'

'O father!' cried Tom, 'I will take care of that; the cart shall be in the wood by the time you want it.'

Then the woodman laughed, and said, 'How can that be? you cannot reach up to the horse's bridle.'

'Never mind that, father,' said Tom: 'if my mother will only harness the horse, I will get into his ear, and tell him which way to go.'

'Well,' said the father, 'we will try for once.'

When the time came, the mother harnessed the horse to the cart, and put Tom into his ear; and as he sat there the little man told the beast how to go, crying out, 'Go on,' and 'Stop,' as he wanted; so the horse went on just as if the woodman had driven it himself into the wood. It happened that, as the horse was going a little too fast, and Tom was calling out 'Gently! gently!' two strangers came up. 'What an odd thing that is!' said one, 'there is a cart going along, and I hear a carter talking to the horse, but can see no one.'

'That is strange,' said the other; 'let us follow the cart and see where it goes.'

So they went on into the wood, till at last they came to the place where the woodman was. Then Tom Thumb seeing his father, cried out,

'See, father, here I am, with the cart, all right and safe; now take me down.'

So his father took hold of the horse with one hand, and with the other took his son out of the ear; then he put him down upon a straw, where he sat as merry as you please. The two strangers were all this time looking on, and did not know what to say for wonder.

At last one took the other aside and said, 'That little urchin will make our fortune if we can get him and carry him about from town to town as a show: we must buy him.'

So they went to the woodman and asked him what he would take for the little man: 'He will be better off with us,' said they, 'than with you.'

'I won't sell him,' said the father, 'my own flesh and blood is dearer to me than all the silver and gold in the world.'

But Tom, hearing of the bargain they wanted to make, crept up his father's coat to his shoulder, and whispered softly in his ear,

'Take the money, father, and let them have me, I'll soon come back to you.'

So the woodman at last agreed to sell Tom to the strangers for a large piece of gold.

'Where do you like to sit?' said one of the men.

'Oh! put me on the rim of your hat, and that will be a nice gallery for me; I can walk about there, and see the country as we go along.'

So they did as he wished; and when Tom had taken leave of his father they took him away with them. They journeyed on till it began to be dusk and then the little man said 'Let me get down. I'm tired.'

So the man took off his hat and set him down on a clod of earth in a ploughed field by the side of the road. But Tom ran about among the furrows, and at last slipped into an old mousehole.

'Good night, masters,' said he, 'I'm off! mind and look sharp after me next time.'

They ran directly to the place, and poked the ends of their sticks into the mousehole, but all in vain; Tom only crawled further and further in, and at last it became quite dark, so that they were obliged to go their way without their prize, as sulky as you please.

When Tom found they were gone, he came out of his hiding-place.

'What dangerous walking it is,' said he, 'in this ploughed field! If I were to fall from one of these great clods, I should certainly break my neck.'

At last by good luck, he found a large empty snail-shell.

'This is lucky,' said he, 'I can sleep here very well,' and in he crept.

Just as he was falling asleep he heard two men passing, and one said to the other,

'How shall we manage to steal that rich parson's silver and gold?'

'I'll tell you,' cried Tom.

'What noise was that?' said the thief, frightened, 'I am sure I heard some one speak.'

They stood still listening and Tom said, 'Take me with you, and I'll soon show you how to get the parson's money.'

'But where are you?' said they.

'Look about on the ground,' answered he, 'and listen where the sound comes from.'

At last the thieves found him, and lifted him up in their hands.

'You little urchin!' said they, 'what can you do for us?'

'Why I can get between the iron window-bars of the parson's house and throw you out whatever you want.'

'That's a good idea,' said the thieves, 'come along, we shall see what you can do.'

When they came to the parson's house, Tom slipped through the window-bars into the room, and then called out as loud as he could bawl,

'Will you have all that is here?'

At this the thieves were frightened and said, 'Softly, softly, speak low, that you may not awaken anybody.'

But Tom pretended not to understand them, and bawled out again,

'How much will you have? Shall I throw it all out?'

Now the cook lay in the next room, and hearing a noise she raised herself in her bed and listened. Meantime the thieves were frightened, and ran off to a little distance; but at last they plucked up courage and said,

'The little urchin is only trying to make fools of us.'

So they came back and whispered softly to him, saying, 'Now let us have no more of your jokes, but throw out the money.'

Then Tom called out as loud as he could, 'Very well: hold your hands, here it comes.'

The cook heard this quite plainly, so she sprang out of bed and ran to open the door. The thieves ran off as if a wolf was at their tails; and the maid, having groped about and found nothing, went away for a light. By the time she returned, Tom had slipped off into the barn, and when the cook had looked about and searched every hole and corner, and found nobody, she went to bed, thinking she must have been dreaming with her eyes open.

The little man crawled about in the hayloft, and at last found a glorious place to finish his night's rest in; so he laid himself down, meaning to sleep till daylight, and then find his way home to his father and mother. But, alas! how cruelly was he disappointed! what crosses and sorrows happen in this world! The cook got up early before daybreak to feed the cows; she went straight to the hayloft, and carried away a large bundle of hay with the little man in the middle of it fast asleep. He still, however, slept on and did not awake till he found himself in the mouth of the cow who had taken him up with a mouthful of hay.

'Good lack-a-day!' said he, 'how did I manage to tumble into the mill?'

But he soon found out where he really was, and was obliged to have all his wits about him in order that he might not get between the cow's teeth, and so be crushed to death. At last down he went into her stomach.

'It is rather dark here,' said he; 'they forgot to build windows in this room to let the sun in, a candle would be no bad thing.'

Though he made the best of his bad luck, he did not like his quarters at all; and the worst of it was that more and more hay was always coming down, and the space in which he was became smaller and smaller.

At last he cried out as loud as he could, 'Don't bring me any more hay! Don't bring me any more hay!'

The maid happened to be just then milking the cow, and hearing some one speak and seeing nobody and yet being quite sure that it was the same voice that she had heard in the night, she was so frightened that she fell off her stool and overset the milk-pail. She ran off as fast as she could to her master, the parson, and said,

'Sir, sir, the cow is talking!'

But the parson said, 'Woman, thou art surely mad!'

However, he went with her into the cowshed to see what was the matter. Scarcely had they set foot on the threshold when Tom called out,

'Don't bring me any more hay!'

Then the parson himself was frightened, and thinking the cow was surely bewitched, ordered that she should be killed directly. So the cow was killed, and the stomach in which Tom lay was thrown out upon a dung-hill.

Tom soon set himself to work to get out, which was not a very easy task; but at last, just as he had made room to get his head out, a new misfortune befell him; a hungry wolf sprung out and swallowed the whole stomach, with Tom in it, at a single gulp, and ran away. Tom, however, was not disheartened, and thinking the wolf would not dislike having some chat with him as he was going along he called out,

'My good friend, I can show you a famous treat.'

'Where's that?' said the wolf.

'In such and such a house,' said Tom, describing his father's house, 'you can crawl through the drain into the kitchen and there you will find cakes, ham, beef, and everything your heart can desire.'

The wolf did not want to be asked twice; so that very night he went to the house and crawled through the drain into the kitchen, and ate and drank there to his heart's content. As soon as he was satisfied, he wanted to get away; but he had eaten so much that he could not get out the same way that he came in. This was just what

Tom had reckoned upon; and he now began to set up a great shout, making all the noise he could.

'Will you be quiet?' said the wolf: 'you'll awaken everybody in the house.'

'What's that to me?' said the little man: 'you have had your frolic, now I've a mind to be merry myself'; and he began again, singing and shouting as loud as he could.

The woodman and his wife, being awakened by the noise, peeped through a crack in the door; but when they saw that the wolf was there, you may well suppose that they were terribly frightened; and the woodman ran for his axe, and gave his wife a scythe.

'Now do you stay behind,' said the woodman; 'and when I have knocked him on the head, do you rip up his stomach for him with the scythe.'

Tom heard all this and said,

'Father, father! I am here, the wolf has swallowed me': and his father said,

'Heaven be praised! we have found our dear child again'; and he told his wife not to use the scythe, for fear she should hurt him.

Then he aimed a great blow, and struck the wolf on the head, and killed him on the spot; and when he was dead they cut open his body and set Tommy free.

'Ah!' said the father, 'what fears we have had for you!'

'Yes, father,' answered he, 'I have travelled all over the world, since we parted, in one way or another; now I am very glad to get fresh air again.'

'Why, where have you been?' said his father.

'I have been in a mouse-hole, in a snail-shell, down a cow's throat, and in the wolf's stomach; and yet here I am again safe and sound.'

'Well,' said they, 'we will not sell you again for all the riches in the world.'

So they hugged and kissed their little son, and gave him plenty to eat and drink, and fetched new clothes for him, for his old ones were quite spoiled.

Jack and the Bean Stalk

Fee — Fie — Fo — Fum

In a little cottage on the banks of a great river there once lived a poor widow who had an only son called Jack. He was not a bad boy at heart, but he disliked work very much, and thought that it was far better fun to paddle or fish in the river, or to go blackberrying and birds' nesting in the woods, than to chop sticks or weed the garden.

One day Jack's mother looked so sad that he asked her what was the matter.

'Alas,' said the poor woman, 'I have no more money in the house, and no more bread. What can I do ? I shall have to sell our good old cow.'

Jack was sorry to hear that the cow must be sold, but he was very anxious to be allowed to sell her himself.

'Let *me* drive her to the nearest town,' he urged, 'It is market day today. And if I call out at the top of my voice, and say that this beautiful black-and-white cow is for sale, all the farmers will crowd around, and offer me any price I please.'

Rather unwillingly, the widow agreed. And then away went Jack, with the cow marching placidly before him, or pausing now and then to nibble the clover and long grass that grew thickly on either side of the road.

Jack had not gone very far before he met a quaint-looking old pedlar who, instead of wearing his hat upon his head, carried it carefully between his two hands.

'Good fortune to you, father,' said Jack. 'The sun is hot – the wind is keen – why don't you wear your hat upon your head?'

'Because, my son,' replied the pedlar, 'I have something in my hat which I prize far more than I do my head.'

So, of course, Jack tried to peep into the hat, but all that he could see inside was a little heap of beans of many different colours.

'Did you ever see beans like *those*?' asked the pedlar.

'No,' returned Jack, 'but they are only beans.'

'That's all you know about it,' said the pedlar.

'What are you going to do with them?' asked Jack, becoming interested. 'Are you going to boil them? Or are you going to plant them in the ground?'

'Neither. I am going to sell them for fifty-five pieces of gold.'

'Are they worth as much as that?'

'They are worth three times more.'

Jack began to think that there must be something very unusual about these beans. They were certainly pretty to look at.

'Harkee, father,' said Jack, 'I have no money – but I am on my way to sell this beautiful black-and-white cow. When I have sold her, I should like to buy those beans of yours.'

'Why wait till then?' replied the pedlar. 'To oblige you, I will take the cow in exchange.'

The bargain was soon clinched. The beans were tilted from the pedlar's hat into Jack's pocket, and away went the pedlar, driving the cow, and away ran Jack, eager to tell his mother how clever he had been.

The widow was surprised to see the boy again so soon, for she did not expect him back till the evening, but when he spread the beans out on the table and told her that he had taken them instead of money for the cow, her surprise changed to dismay, and she burst into tears.

'I am ruined,' she sobbed, 'the poor cow was all I had in the world – and now instead of her you bring me these miserable beans!'

Jack was sorry to see his mother in such distress, but he was still full of the mysterious words of the pedlar.

'Wait a little, mother,' said he, 'these are not ordinary beans. Look, see how pretty they are!'

'I *won't* look!' cried Jack's mother, getting cross. And, with that, she jumped up, and, gathering up the beans in both her hands, threw them out of the open window on to the turf plot outside.

Jack went supperless to bed that night, but he had made up his mind that, as soon as the sun rose next morning, he would go and rescue his precious beans, and take them to the town, and sell them for fifty-five pieces of gold.

Next morning the sun seemed very late in rising. Jack opened his eyes three times, and three times he shut them again, because his little room under the slope of the thatched roof was still dark. The *fourth* time, however, he sat up in surprise, for he saw that the darkness was not black or grey, but *green*. He ran to the window, and he found that it was completely blocked by a gigantic beanstalk, dangling with huge green leaves each about a yard long. The pedlar's beans had sprouted in the night! Evidently they were *not* ordinary beans, after all!

A moment later Jack was out in the garden, and gazing up at the marvellous plant, of which the top was lost in the clouds.

'I'm going up!' said Jack to himself.

And when the widow followed him into the garden all she could see of her son was a pair of patched shoes disappearing among the great green leaves.

Jack was a skilful climber – had he not spent many an hour in the tree-tops that a more dutiful boy would have spent helping his mother to chop, or dig, or sweep? – and the knotted coils of the beanstalk gave him a good foot-hold; but by the time he reached the top, he was out of breath, and had to sit and rest for a while on a fat white cloud, before he felt able to explore the strange place in which he found himself.

In every direction, as far as eye could see, stretched a vast plain of silvery-white sand, broken here and there by clumps of thistles and patches of flints and stones. Jack had had neither supper the night before nor break-fast that morning, and was both hungry and thirsty, but he could see neither well nor pool, house nor orchard, anywhere in sight. The boy's first impulse was to clam-ber *down* the beanstalk as fast as he had clambered *up* it. Then curiosity, and a boyish love of adventure, caused him to change his mind.

'If I explore a bit,' thought Jack, 'I may find a cottage, or an appletree, or a hedge with some filberts in it.'

So he rose from his perch on the cloud, and began to walk across the white sand in a northerly direction, so that the sun should not dazzle him with its brightness. He went *on* and *on*, and *on*, but never a cottage, nor a tree, nor a hedge, did he espy. At last, just when he was beginning to lose heart, he saw, far off, the towers of a great, grim castle, built all of glittering grey rock.

Jack had never seen a castle before, but he thought that it looked like the sort of place where there would be plenty to eat and drink, so he quickened his footsteps, and soon reached the iron-barred door, at which he knocked.

After a few moments the door swung back, and a face peered out, a wonderfully large face, larger than any that Jack had ever seen, for, indeed, it was the face of a giantess.

'Who's there?' asked the giantess, in a gruff voice, 'Come nearer – my eyes are none of the best.'

But Jack didn't go nearer.

'Please, your ladyship,' he said, politely, 'I am only a poor boy – and a very hungry one. Will you not give me something to eat?'

The giantess liked being called 'your ladyship'. So she beckoned Jack to come in, with a finger at least a yard long.

'You shall have a white loaf and a brown loaf,' she promised him, 'but if my husband should come home, you must hide yourself at once, for there is nothing he likes so much for dinner as a roasted boy.'

This sounded alarming, but Jack was a plucky youth, and followed the giantess boldly into the castle. Hungry though he was, he could not eat even *half* of *one* of the huge loaves she set before him; and when he had eaten about a quarter of the white loaf the floor began to quake, and the cups and saucers on the dresser began to rattle, and the giantess cried out in dismay,

'Oh, here comes my husband! Creep into the oven, boy – it is quite cold – and when he falls asleep after dinner you can slip away.'

Jack crept hastily into the oven, and a moment later the giant came striding into the kitchen, sniffing loudly as he came, and roaring,

'*Fee, fi, fo, fum* –
I smell the blood of an Englishman!'

'Nothing of the sort,' returned the giantess. 'What you smell is some nice roast pig that I have got ready for your supper.'

Jack remained very quiet in the oven till the giant had finished his supper, but then he could not resist the temptation to open the door about a quarter-of-an-inch and peep through the crack.

'Wife,' said the giant, 'bring me my pretty little hen.'

The giantess disappeared, and soon returned, carrying a hen with golden-coloured feathers. This hen she placed on the table before her husband, who roared the one word, 'Lay!'

And the obedient hen promptly laid an egg. But it was not an ordinary egg. Jack could see that it was made of solid gold.

After the hen had laid six or seven eggs, the giant and the giantess became drowsy, and before long they were both snoring loudly, with a sound like the very deepest thunder. Then Jack crept very, very softly out of the oven, tucked the pretty little golden hen under his arm, and ran for his life. Across the white sand he ran, taking flying leaps over the patches of rocks and thistles, until

183

he came to the place where the green leaves of the bean-stalk pushed up through the clouds. And then down he clambered, as fast as he could, keeping the hen tucked under his arm all the time.

You may imagine how glad the poor widow was to see her boy again!

'Look, mother,' said Jack, 'I have brought you a hen to make up for the loss of our good old cow!'

'It is a pretty hen,' returned Jack's mother, 'but I will wait and see whether it is a good layer before I stop grieving for my cow.'

Jack set the hen upon the table. 'Lay!' said he.

And at once the obedient hen laid one of her golden eggs.

For a time Jack and his mother lived very contentedly upon the money which they made by selling the eggs of the giant's pretty little hen. Then Jack was seized with a great desire to pay another visit to the grey castle above the clouds. In vain did his mother weep and wail, and beg him to give up so dangerous an idea. He laughed at her fears, and promised that he would bring back with him something at least as precious as the golden hen.

So Jack clambered up the beanstalk again, and soon found his way to the giant's castle, where he knocked boldly at the door.

'Who's there?' asked the giantess, peering out. 'If it's the same rascal of a human boy that came before you, you had better be off!'

'Your Highness,' said Jack, 'if _I_ had annoyed you in any way, do you think I should dare to come back again? Pray give me a crust or two, for I am very hungry.'

The giantess liked being called 'Your Highness'. She stopped frowning and began to smile.

'My eyes are none of the best,' she remarked. 'At first I thought you *were* the boy who stole my husband's pretty little hen. But as you are *not* he, you may come in.'

Jack followed her into the kitchen, and she gave him a piece of gingerbread nearly as big as a small haystack. When he had nibbled off one corner, the floor began to quake, and the cups began to rattle, and the giant's voice was heard roaring,

'*Fee, fi, fo, fum* –
I smell the blood of an Englishman!'

Jack hurriedly crept into a big oaken chest which stood in a far corner of the room, and the giantess assured her husband a few moments later that what he smelt was a nice roast goose which she had ready for his supper.

When the giant had devoured the goose – almost at one mouthful – he said, 'Wife, bring me my money-bags!'

The giantess then brought him two large sacks, one full of golden coins, and one of silver, and while she had a nap by the fire, he amused himself by letting the money run through his huge fingers, and listening to the tinkling it made. Presently he became sleepy, tied up the two bags, and began to snore. Jack, as soon as he heard the thundering sound, softly raised the lid of the chest and got out. And then, seizing a bag under either arm, he ran for his life. When he reached the top of the beanstalk he realised that he could not possibly climb down so heavily laden. So he opened first one sack and then the other, and poured the golden and silver coins down through the clouds before he himself descended.

The widow was amazed to hear the pattering and clinking, and to see the money showering down from the sky. The moment Jack reached the ground, she swore

185

that he must *never* climb the beanstalk again. But Jack only laughed, for in his own mind he had resolved to visit the giant's castle just *once* more.

A few days later, when his mother had gone into the town to do some shopping – for she had plenty of money to spend nowadays – the reckless boy swung himself up the living ladder of leaves and branches, and reached the great plain of white sand for the third time. When he knocked at the giant's door, the giantess seemed afraid to open. 'Go away,' she roared through the keyhole. 'No boys must come here, unless they wish to be killed and eaten!'

'Your Grace,' returned Jack, 'I am not a boy. If Your Grace will look, you will see that I am an aged man!'

And indeed the mischievous fellow had tied a huge beard of snow-white wool on to his chin.

The giantess, who liked being called 'Your Grace', slowly opened the door.

'My eyes are none of the best,' she remarked, 'but you may come in and have a morsel of supper before my husband returns.'

Jack entered the now-familiar kitchen, and listened politely while she told him about the two wicked boys who had come to the castle, and had stolen the giant's treasures.

'*All* boys are rogues and rascals!' declared Jack, solemnly wagging his white beard over the huge currant-bun she had given him.

Presently the ground began to quake and the cups began to rattle.

'Oh!' cried the giantess, 'here comes my husband! Hide, old man, hide in the clock!'

The 'old man' hastily squeezed himself into the case

of the tall eight-day clock beside the hearth, and a moment later the giant himself came stumping in, growling,

'*Fee, fi, fo, fum* –
I smell the blood of an Englishman!'

'No, you don't,' said the giantess. 'What you smell is a joint of beef which I have been cooking for your supper.'

It did not take the giant long to devour the joint of beef. When he had finished, he said, 'Alas, my pretty hen is gone, and my bags of money are gone – but I have one treasure left. Wife, bring me my harp!'

The giantess went to a huge dark cupboard and brought forth a beautiful golden harp which, whenever she set it on the table, began to play the most lovely music all by itself. Very soon both she and the giant were lulled to sleep by the sweet sounds, and then Jack leapt out of the clock-case, snatched the harp from the table, and ran for his life. But the harp was a magic one, and at the touch of Jack's hand it began to cry aloud, 'Master, master!'

Up jumped the giant, rubbing his eyes, and away dashed Jack as fast as he could go.

'Rogue, rascal, thief!' roared the giant, 'it is you who stole my hen and my money-bags! Wait till I catch you!'

But that is just what Jack was determined he should not do.

He was young and nimble, and the giant was old and fat. As swiftly as a deer, he sped over the white sand to the place where the green leaves of the beanstalk pushed up through the clouds. The harp continued to make music and the giant continued to roar all the time.

When Jack was half-way down the beanstalk it suddenly occurred to him that perhaps the harp might stop

playing if he told it to. So he said 'Stop!' and at once the harp obeyed.

In the clouds above him he heard the thudding foot-. steps of the pursuing giant.

'Mother, mother,' called Jack, 'bring me a hatchet, quick, quick!'

Out ran Jack's mother with a big hatchet in her hand.

As soon as he reached the ground, her son began to hack and hew at the beanstalk, and just as the giant reached the top, the hatchet cut clean through the foot. When he saw that he could not possibly climb down the broken beanstalk, the giant uttered a great roar of fury, and turned and went back to his castle, growling and groaning all the way.

But Jack and his mother lived happily ever afterward, and the pretty little hen laid hundreds of golden eggs for them, and the fairy harp made music for them whenever they told it to play.

The roots of the beanstalk withered right away, and as Jack had not kept any seeds, it could not be planted again; nor do I think that there is one like it anywhere in the world today.

Read Me a Story

This is the book for every parent who is wise enough to realise that a child's start in life largely depends on how quickly he is introduced to the reading habit. Some of the contents will be enjoyed by three year olds, much more by four and five year olds; and all by six year olds. How quickly the child begins to read the contents for himself is another matter, for this depends greatly on the patience and skill of the parents. But it will be very surprising indeed if the time lag is too noticeable.

This, then, is a book for children *and* parents to enjoy. There is no Reading Scheme here, no controlled vocabulary, no science at all – just the magic of old and new story-tellers who can set a child's imagination alight.

More Beaver Books

We hope you have enjoyed this Beaver Book. Here are some of the other titles:

Read Me a Story   A Beaver original. A collection of stories and verse for the youngest children, for reading aloud or for the children to read for themselves; edited by Frank Waters

Wilberforce and the Blue Cave   A delightful story for younger readers about Wilberforce the whale and his friends Nelson the crab and Melody the shrimp, who go on holiday to the Mediterranean. By Leslie Coleman, author of *Wilberforce the Whale*, also in Beavers

Journey to the Jungle   A Beaver original. A hilariously funny collection of stories for the youngest readers concerning the adventures of a bus called Livingstone. Written and illustrated by Donald Bisset, author of *This is Ridiculous*, also in Beavers

Rhyme Time   A Beaver original. Over 200 poems specially chosen by Barbara Ireson to introduce younger readers to the pleasures of reading verse. This lively collection is illustrated throughout by Lesley Smith

The Holiday Story Book   A collection of funny and fantastic stories and limericks written and illustrated by Charlotte Hough for younger children

Snail Tale   A charming story about a snail and his friend, an ant, who go off on a journey; written by Avi and illustrated by Tom Kindron

New Beavers are published every month and if you would like the *Beaver Bulletin* – which gives all the details – please send a large stamped addressed envelope to:

Beaver Bulletin
The Hamlyn Group
Astronaut House
Feltham
Middlesex TW14 9AR

376079

Read Me Another Story

Here is a collection which is equally suitable
for reading aloud or for encouraging children
to read for themselves. There is no special
reading scheme or plan to mar the sheer
pleasure provided by good stories – just
traditional fairy tales and nursery rhymes,
poems and limericks, mixed with new and
original material to stimulate the imagination
and provide hours of enjoyment for all.

An expert in the children's book field,
Frank Waters works in publishing and has
edited many anthologies for young people,
including *Read Me a Story*, also published
in Beavers.